HELLRIDER

"Do I look like some kind of lunatic to you?"

"I don't know. But crazy nuts are all I've ever been around. Why did you kill them?" she asked.

"They killed my family. They raped and murdered the woman I would've married. After all the blood over there, all the men I watched die—all I wanted was to get back to something I could call my own, to some sanity. Like you, maybe all I wanted was a real roof over my head and a family I could come home to every night." Heller swallowed again. "But I was cheated. They paid, but maybe I lost more by killing them than I gained. It's a helluva thing to kill a man."

He jumped down on the kick starter and the Harley revved to life.

Also in the *HELLRIDER* series from Pinnacle Books

#1: HELLRIDER

HELLRIDER #2: BLOOD RUN

DAN KILLERMAN

PINNACLE BOOKS NEW YORK

Created by Taneycomo Productions, Inc., in cooperation with Ray Peekner
Literary Agency.

This novel is a work of fiction. Names, characters, places, and incidents
are either the product of the author's imagination or are used fictitiously.
Any resemblance to actual events or places or persons, living or dead, is
entirely coincidental.

HELLRIDER #2: BLOOD RUN

An original Pinnacle Books edition, published for the first time anywhere.

First printing/September 1985

ISBN: 0-523-42590-2
Can. ISBN: 0-523-43538-X

Printed in the United States of America
PINNACLE BOOKS, INC.
1430 Broadway
New York, New York 10018

9 8 7 6 5 4 3 2 1

DEDICATION

This one's for Kathy,
for suffering through
four years of my shit. And
for Jimmy and Johnny D.
They came up with a
couple of good lines.

1

THE MAN NAMED Hell knew trouble when he saw it. It was a sixth sense, an uncanny perception he had honed like a razor's edge long ago in the steaming, bloody cauldron of Southeast Asia. Now a warning bell sounded its silent alarm in the recesses of Jesse Heller's mind as he thundered the black 1200cc Harley-Davidson chopper down the long, empty stretch of backcountry mountain highway toward the isolated woman hitchhiker.

She had her thumb out, but dropped her arm as the black-garbed biker closed the gap. Heller could read her suspicion and fright even from fifty yards out. A blast of chilly wind swirled down from the jagged ridges of the Davis Mountains, seeming to cut like a knife through the scuffed leather of his well-worn jacket. Black clouds rolled over the distant sawtooth peaks, blotting out the sun as the storm belt pushed in from the Pacific. The wind strengthened with each passing moment. It rustled through pine and spruce trees like whispered epitaphs and breathed dust balls across the broad, arid plain that stretched away from the foothills.

The cold air whistled in his eardrums in a painful, steady rush, slapping against his dirt-smeared sunglasses. Heller downshifted. He rolled twenty feet past the woman and braked on the gravel shoulder. A plume of dust thinned behind him. He felt the big engine shoot strong vibrations through his sore legs and rump.

He twisted around to see her and discovered that she looked every bit as wild and beautiful as he had first suspected. And every bit as distrustful.

She stood five and a half feet tall in frayed brown moccasins. Hands on hips, she kept her body cocked toward the lone biker, a pensive look on her face that suggested she might run off into the brush. A large black leather purse hung from her left shoulder, touching her firm, rounded buttocks. She looked as if she had been poured into her skin-tight blue jeans.

The wind blew through her shoulder-length sandy hair and swept it away from her high-cheekboned, smooth-skinned face. Her blue eyes, set wide apart, glinted with a latent hunger, but with the wariness of someone who had known bad times. Heller noted that she wore nothing beneath her white sweater. Her nipples jutted out as if daring the man to touch them. He felt a sudden warmth in his loins as the silence stretched tighter and tighter between him and the woman. It was the bruise beside her full, slightly upturned lips that told Heller all was not well with her.

"Well, you want a ride or not?"

The breeze swept in from the plain, cool and strong. Her nipples seemed to grow, appeared to needle through the sweater as the wind gathered force. She looked at the stocks of the .460 Weatherby rifle and Smith & Wesson 12-gauge jutting from black leather scabbards.

"Look, lady, I know I'm not any knight in shining armor. But there's a storm coming, and I don't plan on getting caught out in it. So what's it gonna be?"

Her mouth hinted at a frown, and a cynical look crept into her eyes. She nodded, then moved toward the idling chopper. Her moccasins crunched gravel. She brushed windswept strands of hair off her face, threw her head back. For a moment she studied the lump on his jaw, the bruise under his right eye, the American-flag patch on the jacket's right shoulder.

"Just what I was looking for," she said. "Another bike bum."

Heller faced front, put the bike in gear and ignored her. His jaw tightened.

"Who lit into you?" she asked as she climbed onto the buddy seat and grasped the sissy bar.

The big chopper lurched away, spitting chunks of gravel.

"My grandmother," he told her.

Three members of the Sinners outlaw motorcycle gang lounged on their choppers in the clearing off the highway, waiting for the chapter road captain to relieve himself behind a pine tree. The bottom rocker on the backs of faded, sleeveless denim jackets declared their chapter as San Angelo, and their club emblem was a black, upside-down crucifix with a yellow Jesus.

They were bearded, long-haired outlaws, all in their late twenties. One Sinner, a tall, skinny, humpbacked outlaw called Igor, sat with his hands on his thighs, bony knees poking out from torn, grease-crusted Levi's. Another outlaw loafed on his hog, his glassy, bloodshot eyes almost hidden by eyelids drooping from the effects of a hashish joint. The other one-percenter slouched against the sissy bar of his black Triumph, cradling the military full-auto Uzi submachine gun as if it were a new toy.

The splatter of urine on tree bark seemed to go on forever.

The wind sprayed yellow piss back onto Bo's leg.

Dark clouds folded like a bubbling pit over the outlaws.

"You gotta lay off them uppers, Bo," Igor griped. He spat and picked at his nose with a dirt-grimed finger. "Twice in the last hour you've had to stop and take a leak. Rest stops are just killin' time, man."

The dope-smoking Sinner took a deep drag and snickered at something only he found amusing. The name Smoky was tatooed on his hairy left forearm.

Bo Stilson tramped from between the pine trees and pulled up the zipper on his dust-and-oil-caked Levi's. Twigs snapped under the heavy steps of his black, chain-wrapped bike boots. His dark eyes glared at the outlaw with the Uzi. "Put that damned thing away, Sniddy," he snapped, moving for his chopper. "You been playing with it all day like it was your pecker."

An odd smile twisted Sniddy's lips. He shoved a clip into the Uzi.

"We gotta get our shit together," Stilson said in a hoarse, strained voice. There was an anxious look on his square, bony, weather-beaten face, a dangerous glint in his wide-eyed gaze. His hands shook as they pulled out a small white container from his jacket. He dumped two amphetamines in his hand, threw them in his mouth, then washed the pills down with a long chug from his canteen. He ran a hand through long black hair that was thin around a high forehead, then tapered back. He had a large, beaked nose that helped make him look like a buzzard.

Igor and Sniddy looked at each other. Smoky blew out a line of pungent hash smoke.

"Bro, we know you're uptight. Man, it's a helluva thing to have to snuff your old lady," the hunchback said. "I always thought she was a pretty righteous chick."

"She ain't righteous no more," Sniddy pointed out.

Wild-eyed, Stilson jolted his head around. His breath rasped through his nostrils. He looked set to explode.

"Easy, man, I didn't mean nothin'," Sniddy said quietly. He looked away from the simmering Sinner road captain.

A sudden hush built up between the two men.

"Let's ride, Bo," the hunchback said, breaking the brittle silence. "Rain's comin' in. Don't none of us wanna get our scoots wet."

Stilson nodded. He dropped down hard on his chopper. He had a patch with 666 on the left shoulder and *Fuck You* tattooed on his right arm. "Fuck her," he growled. "We don't snuff the cunt, Buzz'll do more than just strip our colors."

Smoky took one last drag, then flicked the stub away. "Why don't we all just chill out, bros. Everything's gonna be cool."

Boots came down on kick starters. Choppers roared to life. The bikers fell into pairs and shot down the highway. Peals of thunder roared from their tailpipes.

The black sky echoed a rumbling reply.

It had been a long time since Jesse Heller had known a woman. And even longer since he had loved one. Life had changed him in one lightning-bolt moment of brutality, and the memories had haunted him day and night, had driven him in a tormented, relentless search until he had destroyed the murderers of his family and fiancée. But his quest for vengeance had taken its toll, claimed its price on his life. For he would never again know the things that others took for granted. He would never know luxury, comfort, the security of a job and three square meals, the feel of a soft, warm bed at night. He had abandoned his own freedom in the name of justice and had become a renegade bounty hunter with nobody to turn to and nowhere to run. He knew that every day he lived could well be his last, but that if he was doomed to die a violent death, then he would fend it off for as long as possible. There was only way he was heading out—pumped full of lead or flying over the high side. He lived with the knowledge of this, accepted the fear. Fear was something, though, that could be used like a tool to make a man strong, courageous, able to win against terrible odds. Fear was something he had learned to live with in the war. Fear was now something Jesse Heller could not live without, for he knew that the complacent man went nowhere; he did nothing; he died a slow, insidious and far more terrible death than the one that he knew awaited him at the end of his blood journey.

But the future hadn't arrived. It was something Jesse Heller wasn't immediately concerned about. For, despite a nagging reservation about his passenger, it felt good to have a woman near, riding up against his backside as they rolled down the empty highway together, oblivious for the moment of the wind blasting into him. They had ridden for several miles in total silence. But even if she had spoken, the roar of the engine and the gale-force rush of air would have swept away the sound of her voice.

They came to a bend in the road. The chopper cut between a long line of barren black hills. Beyond the hills Heller saw a service station. He pulled in beside the lone gas pump, beneath a cracked wooden sign that creaked in the breeze and read GAS.

Chickens squawked beside the dilapidated garage. The

rusted ruins of an old model Ford pickup and a black Buick
sedan sagged on dead tires next to the building. A hound dog
with deep-set, watery eyes lay stretched out on the concrete
stoop in front of the station door. It raised its head lazily and
greeted the man and woman with a mournful bark, then lowered its sad face to its paws.

Heller shut off the engine, kicked down the stand and un-
screwed the gas cap. The woman dismounted and stretched
her legs. She looked around at the black, decrepit station. She
crossed her arms over her chest, shivering against the wind
that blew in from the close foothills.

"What a dump," she muttered.

As Heller took the pump and stuck the nozzle in the tank,
a cowbell rang. He heard the station door squeak open.

"How you all doin'?"

Both Heller and the woman looked at the man as he wiped
his hands with an oil-blackened rag. The lean, six-foot-tall
station owner stepped over the hound dog and crammed the
rag in the pocket of grease-splattered blue jeans that looked
several sizes too big. A wide smile stretched across his deeply
lined face, showing chipped, yellowed teeth. The nose of a
Jack Daniel's bottle protruded from his back pocket. He could
have been anywhere from forty to sixty years old.

Heller cocked a half grin as he eyed the man through his
dark shades.

The woman, leery, took a step backward away from the
man.

"Just fine, thanks," Heller said as he filled the tank, then
put the hose back. "You got anything to eat in there?"

The owner shook his head. He pursed his lips. "Nope, not
really, 'less you all like Jerky sticks. There's a diner up the
road. Right off the interstate, headin' west. Bessie there
serves the best danged chili con carne I ever ate. Feel it all
the way down to your toes. The gas, that is." He cackled—
a harsh, raucous sound.

The woman turned away, frowning.

Heller, a sardonic twist to his lips, peeled off a five-dollar
bill and handed it to the man.

"Be back with your change in a sec there, partner."

"You cold?" Heller asked as he saw the woman shivering. The cowbell rang again.

"No. I'm just delighted."

Heller drew a breath. "Look, lady. I don't know what your problem is, but I'm getting tired of the tough-chicken act, okay?"

She glared at Heller and suddenly stopped shaking. Anger flared in her eyes.

"You want to stay here with pop until something better comes along, you're welcome to."

The cowbell sounded once again.

"I'm sorry," she blurted, turning her gaze off Heller.

"Couldn't find my cash drawer there for a minute," the owner explained, stepping toward Heller and the woman. "Not often folks get by this way. Here you are, sonny," he said, handing Heller his change.

"Thanks." Heller stuffed the money in his pocket.

"Sure thing, partner," the owner said as he slipped a key into the pump and reset the gauge. He admired the chopper as Heller mounted and flipped back the kickstand with his boot. "Real fine-lookin' hog there," he said in a quiet voice. Then his eyes fixed on the walnut stock of the high-powered rifle. A pensive look crept into his eyes for a moment. He nodded and walked away. "Take care, folks." He waved.

Heller jumped down on the kick starter. The engine caught; he cranked the hand throttle and revved the engine.

The woman just stood by the chopper. She looked at Heller. For a moment her troubled stare wandered toward the highway they had traveled. Then she slid onto the buddy seat and looked up at the black sky.

"We're not going to get rained on, are we?"

"Not if we make that diner." He could feel her trembling behind him as the breeze whipped through the station, kicking up pieces of trash. "Here. Put this on." He unzipped his jacket, pulled it off and handed it to her.

She slipped into the leather jacket. The arms were too long and the front hung from her like a large sack. She looked at the American flag sewn to the shoulder. "What's the flag patch for?"

"I was in Vietnam," Heller said in a quiet, solemn voice as he put the chopper in gear. The iron horse rolled away with a deafening blast of engine noise.

The sky boiled a dark, billowing mass of clouds.

Thunder cannoned and sheet lightning ripped across the barren plain as the renegade bounty hunter and the strange blond hitchhiker shrank in the distance down the windswept highway.

2

*T*HE CLOUDS BURST and the rain drove down.

The four Sinners rolled down the highway on their choppers—gray, hunched-over shapes that parted the torrent in silence as the storm drowned the engine noise.

They rounded a bend and saw the service station. Rain lashed at them like needles jabbing into their pinched faces and threatening to poke out their squinting eyes. Liquid hammerheads pounded unprotected skulls.

Stilson downshifted, turned and rolled his chopper into the station lot. The other three followed, pushing through the gray downpour to brake in front of the stoop. The rain made a deafening splatter against the asphalt.

The Sinners dismounted.

Stilson pushed through the door.

The cowbell alerted the station owner and brought him from out of the room behind the short wooden counter.

"Fuck. Fuck," Smoky bitterly griped, shaking the water from his long, matted hair like a shaggy dog after a bath.

"Hey, man, watch that," Sniddy growled as water sprayed his face.

"How you all doin'?" The station owner swallowed as he stood stiffly in the doorway of his room. A crumpled nude pinup hung on the green paint-chipped wall beside him. The

9

young, naked model stood in red high heels with straps around the ankles. She posed with her white, well-rounded buttocks showing, her legs splayed to give a full view of her muff. There was a laughing expression on her face, a taunting glint in her blue eyes.

Smoky walked in front of the counter, boots squishing. His red-rimmed, bloodshot eyes stared at the selection of candy bars, mints and gum.

The hound dog lifted its head and looked out at the room from beside a rusted water fountain. The hound's glassy eyes seemed to watch the outlaw biker as he picked through the assorted goods.

Stilson stamped his boots, the chains rattling around the scuffed leather.

Water poured off the four outlaws to form puddles on the cracked tile. Thunder boomed. Lightning flashed in the lot behind the tall Sinners. They loomed in front of the window like grim-faced gargoyles.

"Anybody been by this way, pop?" Stilson asked. He kept his voice low, his tone controlled, but his eyes burned, wide, red, glazed from the effects of speed. He smoothed back his stringy shoulder-length hair with several nervous strokes. Water dripped off his beard.

The owner gazed at Stilson and the other outlaws flanking him. He gave Stilson a sharp nod, as if he had a spastic nerve in his neck. "Yeah, there was, matter of fact. Guy come by here, oh, I'd say less than fifteen minutes ago. Had a gal with him."

"Yeah?" Stilson prodded. His expression darkened.

"Heck, I dunno who he was," the owner explained, sounding as if he was prepared to defend himself.

Anger grew in Stilson's stare. "Well, what did she look like?"

"Blond gal. Real pretty. Tight blue jeans. White sweater."

Stilson's nostrils flared. Now the anger in his eyes became naked, threatening. He looked away from the owner but listened as the man babbled on.

"I thought maybe they was arguin' when I came in to get

his change. Saw she had a bruise on her mouth like maybe he'd beat on her."

The four Sinners fixed hard-eyed gazes on the man.

"Funny thing about him," the owner went on, lowering his voice. "Acted right friendly enough and all, but he had this long, bony, scary-lookin' face. Like one of them death's skulls, you know. Saw some bruises too, like he'd been cracked a few. And he had these guns on his bike—a big ole black Harley hog, twelve hundred cc's of iron." He smiled. "Yeah, I know my bikes. But I got to thinkin' about them after they left. I mean, there was somethin' about this guy that just looked like trouble. Dressed all in black, had this flag patch."

"All right, all right," Stilson said. His face drained of color. His stare widened and his eyes strained from the sockets.

Sniddy looked at Stilson. A nervous tic worked under his left eye. "The son of a bitch that took out Silvers' boys."

"Damn," Stilson breathed. "Damn!" he rasped. The soft flesh beside his windpipe pulsed. "Which way they head?"

The owner's mouth opened, but no words sounded for a moment. "They headed north. Asked for somethin' to eat, so I told them to go to Bessie's. That's a diner off Ten."

"Bo, you think it's him?" Igor asked, his voice trembling.

"Hell, if it is," Sniddy said, his lips curled back over his teeth, "he's only one dude. One lone fucking dude. We can snuff him out easy. Not only that, Bo—he's got your old lady."

Stilson raised his arm and waggled his hand. He appeared to struggle with a thought. "Slinky was one of Silvers' whores. Remember how she came crawling back to Boone and them last week all sorry? Right after the funeral. Told us all about this Heller. How he snuffed out a whole bunch of Stalkers and Burton's chapter. Blew them up. Charred them all to a crisp. Burned down the sluthouse."

"Heck, that's all they been jawin' about on the radio last few days," the owner said. Spittle ran down his lips. "Couldn't of been him. Naaaah. I heard the guy that done it was dead."

Stilson's look became flint hard. "Well, you heard wrong, pop."

"What do you wanna do, Bo?" Igor asked.

Stilson turned his head, his expression as sharp as broken glass. "We're gonna nail him to a black Sinners' cross, that's what we're gonna do. Smoky," he snapped, "want you to ride back to Buzz. Tell him we got the bitch, and tell him we found the dude that did in Silvers too. He'll want to know."

"Aw, shit, piss, Bo. It's a long bitchin' haul back to Sherwood. And in the fuckin' rain. Man, c'mon."

"Cut your whinin', Smoky. Just do it. Buzz is gonna want to know about this. We're talking about outlaw pride, man. Where the hell's yours?"

Smoky's lips flapped as he hissed out a long breath.

"We lost some good boys with the Stalker bunch," Sniddy reflected, eyes fixed in a cold stare between Stilson and the hunchback.

"You're damned right-on we did," Stilson said. "Some of the best buddies I had. You know how much class snuffing this bastard would earn us?" Stilson's eyes bulged as if he was fantasizing about the kill and the glory that would follow.

"So what are we pissing around here for?" Sniddy rasped.

Stilson glared at Sniddy. Then Stilson wheeled, throwing open the door. Wind and rain blasted past the outlaws.

Smoky crammed a handful of candy bars into his pants pocket and headed for the door.

"Hey," the owner protested as Smoky's hand touched the door handle.

The voices of Stilson and Sniddy were muted by thunder as Smoky turned, locking gazes with the owner.

The owner faltered and he suddenly looked pathetic. He shrugged and a nervous smile flickered over his lips. "I gotta make a living, you know."

Contempt shadowed Smoky's features for an instant. Then he smiled and reached into his pocket. "Sure, man," he said as he flipped a wadded ball of cash on the counter. "No hard feelings, huh?"

The owner unraveled the rumpled cash as the bikers went

out into the rain. He held two one-dollar bills, one of which was almost torn in half. He looked through the door glass at the bikers and frowned.

"Put your skullbuckets on," Stilson ordered as he fastened the helmet strap under his chin. He mounted his chopper and jumped down on the kick starter. "Listen to me!" he shouted against the din of engine noise, rolling thunder and crashing rain. "If they're at this diner, I don't want no witnesses."

"Why don't you wait until this rain passes?" Smoky yelled. "They ain't goin' nowhere in this." His hair hung in knotted coils from his head.

Heavy raindrops splatted off their black helmets as the other three fired up and gunned their engines. Their faces were grim with determination as they pulled away from the stoop and headed slowly away from Smoky.

"Ah, fuck you," Smoky bitched, mounting his Harley. He put on the Nazi helmet he had stolen from a White People Power rally in Austin. Red swastikas and *fuck off* were painted on the sides of the helmet.

Smoky dropped down hard in the saddle and stomped his boot on the kick starter. He revved the engine and shot across the parking lot. The rain slashed at his face. He winced and cursed. He hit a puddle and a spray of water slapped his face. As he started his turn out of the lot, the bike slipped out from under him as if he'd been on sheer ice. Instinctively, he pushed away, drew his elbows close to his body and tucked up into a ball as the chopper tumbled. His helmet banged off the asphalt and flew off his head. A harsh grunt of pain sounded from deep in his chest as he slammed into the ground. He slid behind his spinning chopper and went out of the lot and halfway across the road, parting the slick surface of water like an eel. His jacket and pants sponged up the wetness while his slide spurted out water.

The faint grind of chopper engines reached his ears. He clambered to his feet and looked in anger at his three outlaw brothers as they vanished in the distance behind a falling curtain of rain.

Smoky looked at his downed Harley. He turned and kicked his helmet halfway across the station lot.

The Harley's front tire touched the concrete partition in front of the long diner window. Heller shut off the engine and leaned the chopper on its kickstand. The woman hopped off the seat and jogged out of the hissing rain to the protection of the diner's awning.

Heller followed her into the diner. The clamor of raindrops against the awning was softened by the loud volume of the television set that hung from the wall at the end of the counter. The newscaster was talking about a terrorist hijacking in the Middle East.

Two burly, solemn-faced men turned halfway around on their counter stools. They studied the woman first, appreciating the long, shapely legs underneath her soaked, clinging jeans. Then they looked at Heller and turned around, dismissing him with smug expressions.

"Over there," Heller quietly told the woman and nodded to indicate a booth in the far corner. He heard the sound of plates breaking in the kitchen.

"Jeez, Louise, Barney, what's with all that racket back there, for chrissakes?" a short, plump, dark-haired waitress called out in a raspy, high-pitched voice. She strode around the end of the counter, jotting down an order on a note pad.

Heller felt the other customers' eyes on his back as he and the hitchhiker threaded their way through the cramped tables and chairs in the small dining area.

They slid into a booth and Heller took in his surroundings with a raking once-over look.

The newscaster's voice seemed to boom through the diner, muffling the rain rattling on the one long window. The man talked about the President's new plan to reduce taxes and cut federal spending.

The spicy aromas of hot chili peppers made Heller aware of the hunger pangs that clawed at his empty stomach.

The waitress walked up to the booth. After she had taken their order and gone back to the kitchen, Heller and the woman sat in silence.

Heller slicked back his short black hair and felt the water

trickle down his back beneath his drenched black undershirt and into his pants. The skin on his corded forearms pimpled from the chill of his wringing-wet clothes. He studied the woman closely for a moment. She seemed distracted, her gaze wandering around the diner.

"You all right?"

She looked at him but quickly turned her face away from the piercing scrutiny of his blue-green eyes. "I'm just fine. Thank you." She paused. "I just have some things on my mind."

"You never told me your name."

"Lisa. Lisa Stephens."

The waitress came back and set down two saucers and cups. Steam wafted from the rich-looking black coffee.

Heller poured cream in his coffee. "I'm Jesse." He tore open two sugar packets.

Lisa Stephens looked at the lean, muscular, black-garbed man with the high forehead and lean, skeletal face as if noticing him for the first time. She looked away from Heller. "Where were you going? If you don't mind my asking."

He took a sip of coffee. "I'm not sure. West, I suppose. How about you? If you don't mind my asking."

She let out a soft sigh. She turned her eyes away from Heller, focused her attention on the cup of coffee. "I'm not too sure at this point. Would you excuse me for a minute," she said abruptly and pushed herself up out of the booth.

"Sure." Heller lifted the cup to his lips. His brow creased, he watched the blonde as she padded over the tile in her moccasins toward the rest rooms. He found her nervous, aloof. She seemed frightened but tough, capable of handling herself. He remembered how she had called him a bike bum, recalled their exchange at the gas station. But his thoughts were interrupted by the newscaster's voice, and Heller shifted his gaze toward the television set.

"Dallas Police officials announced today that the man wanted in connection with last week's killings of members of the Death Stalkers and Satan's Avengers outlaw motorcycle gangs is still at large. So far, several charred bodies have been accounted for in the remote desert region near . . ."

"Can you believe that guy?" Heller heard one of the customers at the counter ask the other one. The customer shook his head in disbelief. "All the trouble they've had down at Swedie's over the years with that bunch of riffraff. You ask me, the sons of bitches finally got what they deserved. Personally, I'd like to give the guy a medal."

"Anybody take on a bunch of bikers like that is either crazy or stupid. Or got some pretty damned big balls."

Heller's attention was divided between the broadcast and the two men.

"Hey, fellas, the mouth, huh," the waitress chided, her face twisted in a scowl. She reached for the television and lowered the volume.

"C'mon, Bessie, don't turn it down now. They got the sports on next."

"You can hear it just fine. I got other customers, you know, for chrissakes. Paying customers. You two just been sitting around here all afternoon wiping out the coffee supply."

"Yeah, Charlie, relax. She's gotta be able to hear Barney busting dishes all over the kitchen."

The two men laughed. Heller looked away from the counter as Lisa Stephens dropped down into the booth. She had washed and dried her face and brushed her hair. Her wet, frizzy tangles rested on the jacket's shoulders.

They sat in awkward silence for several seconds before the woman spoke.

"You say you're heading west?"

Heller nodded. "Most likely."

She seemed to contemplate something for a moment. "Can I ride with you to Arizona? I can pay for gas and food. I have some friends in Tucson. I can give you more money when I get there."

A half smile touched Heller's lips. He shook his head gently. "That's all right. You don't have to do all that. Not if I end up headed that way. And it looks like I am."

"I insist. On paying my way, that is."

Heller looked at her, searching her face. His relaxed

expression hardened into a look of brooding thought. "Okay. Whatever you like. I'll take you as far as I'm going."

She let out a quiet breath as she looked away from Heller. "But do you mind telling me what it is you're running from?"

Her head snapped up. She shot him a startled, angry look.

"Just in case I happen to get caught up in some mess," he explained. "I don't like surprises."

"I'm not running from anybody or anything. And even if I was, it's none of your business anyway."

Heller worked his jaw, glanced at his coffee. When he looked back at her, there was impatience in his eyes. "I suppose you've noticed the bruise on your mouth."

She stayed silent for a long moment. "My old man did that," she conceded in a bitter voice, her face tight with controlled anger. "My ex-old man."

"Who's a biker."

She showed Heller a smirk. "Well. So what are you? You just said that like you ride some kind of golden Trojan horse."

Heller gestured with his hands. "Just trying to find out a little something about you, that's all. No need to be so testy."

"Well, don't be asking questions. I don't plan on getting friendly, cowboy."

Heller nodded. An odd grin turned up the corner of his lips. "How did you get so tough?"

"Look," she said, softening her tone, "I was just getting sick and tired of the whole stinking biker scene. That's what the problem was. It was nowhere. And I've been nowhere all my life, cowboy. I got tired of being an *old lady*. I got tired of seeing the same people stoned out of their minds every single night until they didn't know their own names." Her words rushed together, the frustration grinding into her tone until her voice cracked. "I got tired of hogs and runs and mamas and trains." She looked at Heller, anger burning into her stare. "I was threatened with having to pull a train. I was beaten because I let the old man's beer run out. This didn't happen just once in a great while."

"So why did you let yourself get involved?"

"I don't know," she sighed. She slouched as if the bad

memory were a physical force that dragged her deeper into her misery. "I guess it looked good at the time. I ran away from my stepmom's at sixteen; that was twelve years ago. I was broke, and along comes this dude who looks freer than the breeze."

They sat in silence for long moments. The television sportscaster, the voices of the two men at the counter and the talk of the people around the diner were one jumbled maze of noise in his ears as he withdrew into the dark caverns of his tortured memory. He remembered a time long ago when he had a brother, a father, a stepmother. He saw the face of the woman who had loved him, who had waited patiently, longingly, for his return from Vietnam so they could marry.

"More coffee?"

Heller, jarred loose from his private torment by the waitress' voice, looked up and saw her standing next to him with a full pot of coffee.

The rain and the wind drove against the long window at the front of the diner. The loud, rattling noise muted the approach of the three choppers rolling across the parking lot.

Lisa Stephens lifted her face up from her hand and peered past the waitress as she filled Heller's cup.

"What's the matter?" Heller saw the fear spread over the woman's face, then heard the choppers.

Three blurred figures, darkened by the water sliding down the window, swung off the big bikes. Heller leaned back to get a clear view of the door and saw the shadowy figures grab objects from their saddles. He came to the stark realization of what they were grabbing.

He looked back at Lisa Stephens and felt his stomach knot from the fear that crawled through him. The blonde opened her mouth. A desperate, helpless expression formed on her face, as if she was going to implore something of Jesse Heller.

The door crashed open, splintered by a thundering boot heel. It banged into the wall, shattering its glass pane.

There was a split second of stunned silence as the three

heavily armed Sinners poured through the doorway. Wind and rain gusted into the diner with them.

Heller saw the crazed, wild-eyed look in Bo Stilson's eyes. He grabbed Lisa Stephens by the shoulder as the snout of an Uzi submachine gun swung toward them.

The waitress screamed in terror.

"You fuckin' cunt!" Stilson yelled and opened fire.

3

*H*ELLER'S RIGHT FOREARM shot up, cracking onto the table's edge and flipping it over an instant before Stilson's finger squeezed the Uzi's trigger. The roar of the submachine gun cut off the Sinner's shouted curse, and a burst of 9mm Parabellum slugs sprayed the back of the dining area. Sniddy slid beside the outlaw road captain and let his own Uzi rip loose with a deafening hail of wood-churning, glass-shattering rounds.

But Heller moved like a wink of lightning, driven by the adrenaline that coursed through his body like wildfire. He pulled the blonde behind him. Using his body as a shield, he punched into the waitress as the twin lines of fire swept toward them and blew the glass coffeepot out of her hand. They tumbled behind the counter in a tangle of arms and legs. Chunks of Formica countertop, glass slivers and shredded cakes and doughnuts blew over their heads and splattered the wall.

One of the two men at the counter dove over it, his legs kicking cake trays into the wall while the other man rushed the shotgun-wielding Igor in the doorway. Igor spun, slammed the barrel of his Remington 12-gauge into the charging man's face and knocked him back into the counter. Blood pumped from the man's split nose. His head smacked

20

the Formica edge with a sound like a melon dropping from a great height.

A tall, potbellied man in a soiled white apron and a stained undershirt popped out from behind the kitchen door and leveled a small-caliber revolver at the bikers. But the chattering Uzis swung around and stitched the cook with double lines of flesh-eaters, spinning him around in a death dance. The Remington 12-gauge roared and blasted open the man's back in a bloody cloudburst.

The black-helmeted, grim-faced Sinners stood side by side and raked the counter with streams of slugs that punched out refrigerator doors, exploded milk cartons and food containers and peppered the wooden wall. Sniddy's eyes widened, his crazy laughter drowned by the roaring relentless decimation.

The din reached an ear-piercing crescendo. Heller lifted his head and glass splinters jabbed into his exposed flesh. He felt the blonde trembling behind him, but it was the waitress he saw first. He stared into her empty, glazed-over eyes. A trickle of blood ran down from her forehead. He winced. *Damn! Why did the innocent always have to get hurt?*

Heller rolled over. He snatched Lisa Stephens' arm in a viselike grip and heard her cry out.

"Move it!" he rasped. Crab-walking on his hands and knees, he dragged the woman away from the slug-ravaged counter, from the whine of ricocheting bullets.

And as suddenly as they had opened fire the two Sinners released the Uzi triggers. They stood like statues for long moments as wisps of grayish-white smoke curled from the snouts of the submachine guns. The silence seemed to trap the sound of a glass shard that tumbled from the refrigerator door and shattered on the tile.

Igor pumped the shotgun's action, jacking a live cartridge into the breech. The empty shell spun from the ejector port and clattered off the tile.

Stilson stepped across the room, kicking a bullet-splintered chair out of his way. Sniddy moved away from the window. The unconscious man slumped against the counter, suddenly slid along the Formica-reinforced front and toppled on his side between two stools.

Igor's hair hung out the back of his helmet, whipping around in the wind that came through the door. He raised the goggles off his eyes.

Stilson reached the end of the counter and stood over the dead woman. The Uzi clenched in his right hand hung low by his side. He surveyed the carnage.

"Where the fuck is that bitch?"

Jesse Heller ignored the cold rain that slashed his face as he rounded the corner of the diner, hauling Lisa Stephens behind him.

Heller reached his Harley and released the woman. He slid the short-stocked, sawed-off Smith & Wesson 12-gauge from its scabbard. Pumping the slide action, he swung the barrel up and braced the stock against his hip.

"Get down!"

Heller's face hardened with a look of savage intent. His eyelids narrowed against the driving rain, he peered through the water-rippled window for a split second. Making out the fuzzy shape of Stilson, he squeezed the trigger and blasted out the large windowpane.

Stilson dove to the floor behind the counter as huge shards of glass razored across the diner.

Sniddy wheeled and triggered a short burst that punched off jagged glass strips from the shattered window opening. The Uzi's magazine emptied and he vaulted over the counter and disappeared behind the other side.

Heller cocked the action, turned and fired. The blast seemed to part the rain before it sheared off a chunk of doorjamb. Igor showed near the doorway, jumping back as the wood exploded.

"Start it up!" Heller yelled, cocking the slide. He whirled and unleased another round through the window.

The woman flinched at the roar but dropped down on the seat and flipped on the ignition as Heller pumped another round into the chamber.

He spun left. The shotgun bucked in his hands and a 12-

gauge scatter-burst of double-ought buck thundered into the wall beside the doorway. Debris and glass flew across the diner.

Lisa stamped down on the kick starter. The engine sputtered. "C'mon," she cried, jumping down again on the kick starter.

Heller cannoned another round at Stilson's position. A chunk of counter spit out across the diner. The Harley revved to life and he sidestepped toward it keeping his attention focused on the counter and his smoking scatter gun pointed at the dining room.

Heller sheathed the shot gun, mounted and snapped back the kick starter. He pushed the chopper back with his boots as Stilson rolled out from behind the counter with the Uzi thrust out from under him. The Sinner bounded to his feet, staggering through overturned wreckage.

Sniddy leaped over the counter as Igor strode through the doorway that looked as if it had been chewed up by a swarm of termites.

The three Sinners sprang through the blasted opening and into a gust of wind and rain, firing as the Harley thundered across the lot.

Lisa mashed herself into Heller's backside as bullets ricocheted off the asphalt and a slug blasted the left side-view mirror off the handlebars. Heller leaned forward, bore down and tore across the lot.

Stilson cursed the Uzi when it emptied. He snatched out the dry clip and hurled it after Heller.

Snapping a fresh clip into his Israeli-made subgun, Sniddy hopped on his chopper.

Igor sheathed his Remington and pulled the goggles down over his eyes. He swung onto his hog as Stilson shoved a thirty-round clip into his Uzi and ran to his bike.

He mounted up and the three Sinners kicked their machines into life and roared after their prey.

Rain stung Heller's face like ground glass.

He rolled across the interstate overpass as a car swished underneath. On the far side he braked in the middle of the road and twisted around to look for his pursuers. He found

none. The engine's snarl filled the cold silence between him
and the woman.

"Freer than the breeze, huh?" Heller said in a tight voice.
He gunned the engine as if this would ease his anger. "Sick
and tired of the stinking biker scene, were you? I guess that
was me he was calling a fucking cunt, right?"

The woman sat in silence. She stared at him with a look of
fear and uncertainty as thunder boomed beyond the mist-
shrouded hills.

"What are you going to do?"

"I can't do jackshit against two Uzis, lady," he admitted
grimly. He clenched his teeth as he dropped the big black
Harley into gear and began heading down the long ramp.
Tires sluiced through water that pushed across the road in a
glassy sheet. Heller lurched the bike into high gear. Craning
his head around, he saw two beams of light penetrate the gray
downfall a half mile behind. He raced the black chopper out
onto the interstate.

Seconds later Stilson shot across the overpass and turned
down the ramp. He mouthed a curse as water sprayed up into
his face.

Heller focused intense concentration on the road. He
brought the iron beast up to seventy miles per hour. The hog
shook between his legs as if the earth were shuddering beneath the blur that was his front tire. Wind, rain and asphalt
seemed to rush at his face in a jumbled maze of distorted sight
and sound. He had to keep the bike straight, for under the
conditions he now faced he might as well have been riding
on ice. A sudden turn or jolt, a bump or a shift in weight would
send them both tumbling to a bloody, agonizing death.

Heller looked into the right side-view mirror. The glass in
the mirror shimmied from the thunderous vibrations. The
gray shapes of the outlaw bikers were a good quarter mile
behind.

The Sinners' choppers moved down the ramp, racing to
close the gap on their quarry.

The woman pressed her face into Heller's back, her arms
wrapped tighter around his waist.

The wind shrieked in Heller's uncovered ears. The guardrail was a shimmering white ribbon in the periphery of his vision. He looked at the road through slits, his tearing eyes almost blind from the slap of wind and the pinpricks of rain. He glanced into the side-view mirror.

Stilson closed the gap to a hundred feet, opening up a thousand cubes of engine thunder to full throttle. The outlaw road captain slouched and the gap tightened to seventy-five feet. He stayed wide of the spume Heller's back tire threw back at him.

Heller saw the pothole an instant before he missed it by inches. Ice speared through his guts and his throat constricted. He knew he had just barely escaped his death fall, for potholes became craters at eighty miles per hour.

Stilson blew by the pothole, but Sniddy bounced down into the rut. The handlebars wrenched out of his hands as if the chopper had a mind of its own. The bike toppled, shot out from under the outlaw like a cannonball and plowed into the guardrail.

Sniddy followed his chopper into the railing like a magnetized chunk of steel. His helmet cracked off a metal slat and his skull burst like eggshell. The chopper slid down the rail at more than seventy miles per hour, twisting and bouncing between the slats in a horrendous rending of metal. Lethal projectiles of iron exploded across the highway.

Sniddy's body ripped open on the slats as if the guardrail were one long meat grinder. He splattered down the rail in a spray of blood. Gore splashed as gravel sheared the denim off his back and legs and stripped the flesh off his bones like countless razor blades. His arms snapped like dry pretzels and his left leg cleaved off at the hip and spun out across the road.

The hunchbacked biker watched in horror as his outlaw brother went down. Oblivious to the eighteen-wheeler rolling less than forty feet behind him, Igor braked hard. The bike went out of control, weaving with the sudden application of brakes on the slick surface. It went down, iron scraping over asphalt. Igor rolled screaming just before the tractor trailer crushed him. The fat double tires sucked up the Sinner and churned his body up like a hay reaper, leaving behind a broken, mangled sack that was unrecognizable as something once human.

Heller couldn't see the mayhem in his side glass, but he saw the tractor trailer fall far behind as it slowed. He knew something had happened and that two of the outlaws had gone down. He squinted into the wind and saw the mist thicken in the distance. He knew that it was only a matter of time on this unfamiliar, rain-slippery road at full throttle, until he and the woman ate the asphalt.

"Get my helmet!"

"What?" she shouted.

"My helmet! Saddlebag! Get it out!"

Heller eased up on the throttle, dropping his speed to just under seventy as the blonde dug into the saddlebag. She carefully wriggled the helmet free from under a black leather holster that held a large stainless-steel .44 Ruger New Super Blackhawk magnum.

Heller let Stilson gain on him until the gap was cut to thirty feet. He shifted his weight left with an imperceptible nudge that lined his Harley up in front of the outlaw.

"Here."

Heller hunched low in the saddle, dug his chin into his left shoulder and turned his head a little to tell her, "Drop it when I tell you."

"What?"

"Just let it drop! When I tell you!"

He looked into the mirror, leaned right and eased back on the throttle. He felt the wind lashing at his face, heard it screaming in his ears.

Stilson hit the throttle and shot forward like a torpedo with a crazed look in his eyes. His teeth gritted in a macabre grin.

"Now!"

The black helmet dropped from her hand. Bouncing up from the asphalt, it thudded into Stilson's chest as if it were an iron ball. Heller cranked the throttle and fired off down the road like a high-powered rifle bullet. He cleared himself of Stilson's path as the latter's chopper twisted away from the outlaw and flung itself toward the guardrail. Metal crumpled in at the terrible screeching impact as Stilson flew over the high side. The chopper cartwheeled fifty yards down the shoulder of the road. A saddlebag burst across the highway, spewing its contents in all directions.

Heller let off on the throttle. He came to a long, slow, braking halt, fighting to keep the back wheel from pulling away. He turned the chopper sideways and sat in the middle of the road. The drizzle slanted down from the dark hills in a fine mist that sheeted across the man and woman.

Heller gazed at the debris strewn a hundred yards behind.

The woman turned her stare away from the wreckage and flashed Heller a dark, questioning look.

He slipped the Harley into gear and thundered back toward the ruins of Stilson's chopper. Heller pulled off onto the shoulder, stopped and, leaning the bike on its kickstand, slid off the seat. He stood in front of his idling chopper for a long moment, his grim stare fixed on the wreckage. The pulverized heap that was Stilson's Harley was a hundred feet behind Heller, bits and pieces of engine scattered across the gravel. The sissy bar was crumpled back, almost touching the shredded back tire. The forks were cracked and held the spinning front tire up in the air at a crooked angle.

Lisa Stephens' expression was tight with anxiety. Her nervous eyes darted up at Heller. Her hands shook as she dug into her purse and pulled out a pack of Virginia Slims.

Heller stepped toward the warped rail. He looked at the back of the sign just inside the railing. The thick metal stakes were twisted around, and the sign they held up was bent back on the side where Stilson had hit it.

Heller stopped in front of the battered rail. Stilson's torn body lay at the bottom of the steep, rocky embankment. The outlaw's left arm was bent up behind his back and his head lolled down against his chest from a broken neck.

Heller turned his head and rested a solemn look on the speed-limit marker. He saw the dent, the splotch of crimson.

"He's . . . he's . . ."

Heller looked at the woman. She now stood by the chopper, her hand trembling as she raised the cigarette to her lips.

"Yeah," he told her as he turned away. He saw beer cans

and a black undershirt spread around the saddlebag in the middle of the road. But it was the Uzi that caught Heller's eye. He stepped onto the highway, picked up the submachine gun and examined it. Heller unlatched the magazine, saw the clip was full and shoved it back in.

The blonde flinched as Heller squeezed off a three-round burst across the highway and into the hills.

Heller looked at the Uzi in silent appraisal. The Israeli-made submachine gun was smaller than the standard-issued M-16 he had used in the Army, but it felt a little heavier than a fully loaded M-16. He had heard the Uzi was a reliable, durable weapon, one of the best automatic subguns in the world. He liked the way it looked—sleek, compact, deadly— liked the way it molded into his hands.

Heller scooped up four thirty-round clips. He bent over the saddlebag and stuffed in the clips. He froze as he saw the sticks of dynamite. He looked up, then over at the woman. He stood, clutching the saddlebag. His gaze hardened by the pent-up tension and anger he felt, he walked to his helmet and picked it up with the two fingers of his Uzi-brandishing hand.

"What was your ex–old man doing playing around with dynamite?"

Heller moved across the highway toward his chopper.

The blonde watched him, startled. She dropped her gaze away from Heller's penetrating search and stood shivering with one arm folded over the front of the jacket. "I don't know. I didn't even know he had it."

Heller draped the saddlebag around the sissy bar. He turned and faced the blonde. She kept her back to him and blew out a long stream of smoke. Heller could almost hear her heart pounding.

"Do you want to talk about it now?" he asked, his voice cold and low. " 'Cause you're in it as deep as I am, whether you like it or not. Maybe deeper."

She sucked in a last breath of smoke and flicked the cigarette out into the road. She seemed to ponder something for a moment before she faced Heller.

Heller held out the Uzi. "Here. You hold this."

She hesitated before taking the submachine gun.

"You'd better put this on too," he said, handing her his black helmet.

Heller mounted up and flipped back the kickstand.

Again she seemed reluctant. She looked set to say something but climbed on the buddy seat in silence and rested the Uzi in her lap. She put her moccasins up on the pegs, strapped on the helmet and tugged together the matted blond snarls that hung from the back of the helmet.

Heller felt her shuddering, either in fear or against the cold mist. He put the Harley in gear.

"You don't understand," she said, her voice small against the engine's powerful grind as Heller wheeled around and pulled away from the warped speed-limit marker.

"You're right about that."

4

JESSE HELLER PITCHED a clump of sagebrush into the crackling flames. Then he leaned back against the cold adobe of the crumbled Spanish mission and lifted a spoonful of pork and beans out of his steaming tin plate. The fire hissed out orange tentacles from beneath the charred bark of a cottonwood, consuming the dry, bushy plant in a succession of brittle popping sounds. Smoke curled out, a sweet smell that filled the lone-wolf biker's nose and made his eyes water.

Shadows danced along the rubble behind Lisa Stephens. She hunched close to the fire, shivering in the cold desert night.

The storm had ended, but clouds still covered the sky. The darkness beyond the ruins was as thick as the black maw of a bottomless pit. A low wind whistled along the foothills of the Apache Mountains, cutting through the mission debris and making the flames dance.

A grim-faced Heller looked at the woman's illuminated figure on the other side of the fire as she swallowed a mouthful of food. Heller listened to the fire in the silence. He felt the icy dampness of his wet clothes and trembled, but forced himself to ignore the bitter discomfort of cold air on exposed flesh as the moaning breeze knifed through his cotton and corduroy garb. Heller was concerned with the trouble they'd

left behind; he knew that the future was murky, knew that
tomorrow promised more violence, more bloodshed. A familiar dark feeling nagged him.

He studied the woman for long moments.

"Well," he said. "You haven't said a word since your late
old man ate the road. I'm still waiting for you to tell me
something."

The blond woman had slipped into a state of brooding silence since the brutal deaths of the three Sinners. Her mood
had hardened the farther behind they had left the strewn
wreckage and mutilated bodies. As they had snaked a tortuous path through rugged, barren, hill-cut country, Heller's
patience with the woman and the situation he found himself
cast into had worn thin.

Lisa glowered at Heller.

"Maybe I'm just not ready to talk about it, cowboy,
okay?"

She went back to eating. Scooping food into her mouth,
she sank back into a stony silence and ignored Heller.

The biker peered at her and felt his tolerance evaporate like
the fire's smoke that vanished up into the darkness. He drew
in a deep breath and set the plate down beside himself. He
focused a cold gaze on the woman, his slit-eyed stare reflecting the flames like a pair of black marbles behind glass.

"You know, women like you aren't too uncommon. In
fact, I've met and stomached more than my share."

Her head jolted up. She shot Heller a startled glare.

"Remember how you told me that this guy looked good at
the time when you were flat-assed broke? That little phrase
of yours, *freer than the breeze*, sticks in my mind for some
reason. You know why? Because women like you all want
something different out of life, but you never put a finger on
what it is you want. You just float along, thinking you de-
serve something better just because you've got a nice soft
round ass and flash around a pretty come-to-me smile. You
have this fascination with the renegades and the outlaws and
the guys with the I-don't-give-a-damn-about-tomorrow atti-
tudes. The guys people notice but who everyone admires
from a distance. The guys who can flip off a state trooper and

get away with it. The guys you're creamin' in your panties for but wouldn't dare take home to Daddy.''

Heller saw her shoulders shake, her eyes flare up in silent rage.

''But the going gets tough and you wake up one morning and realize these guys are going nowhere,'' he pressed on, ''or they aren't going where you suddenly think they should go. Then you light out like they never meant a thing, like they never existed. This fantasy of yours wears thin and you split. Yeah, I've seen it, lady. Too many times. When the good times go and there's a little struggle involved, you just walk out the door. It's called fair-weather fuckin'.

''So you end up marrying the accountants and the engineers and five years down the road you realize you don't have it one bit better. You've got that security. You've got that golden pot to crap in. But that's all you've got. You'll still be a miserable bitch, making everyone else miserable because you didn't have the guts to decide what it is you really wanted and go after it.''

She trembled violently. Her face drained of color and her eyes dampened.

''Don't you sit there and judge me, you son of a bitch!'' she snarled as she hurled her plate at Heller's face.

He ducked and the tin plate clattered against the adobe behind him.

Lisa jumped to her feet, set to attack him. Her fists clenched tightly and her arms quivered by her sides.

''Don't you ever judge me by another woman, or anyone else, you arrogant bastard!'' she screamed. ''You don't know what it is I've been through, you worthless piece of biking trash!''

Heller ran the back of his hand over his cheek to wipe off the slop from her thrown food.

''Relax, all right?'' he told her. He looked at her with a steady gaze and let a long breath rasp out his nose. ''I was just trying to get you to come out of your little shell. Didn't know it was so fragile.'' He paused. ''Look, we both know you're hiding something.''

''Aren't we all? What are you hiding?''

"I almost got my head blown off back there because of whatever it is you're hiding. If you ride with me, you level about that mess we left. Fair enough?"

She stood and glared down at Heller through the crackling fire. Finally she crouched, dropped hard on her rump and stared into the flames with a dark, morose expression. She drew her knees up to her chest and folded her arms around them. Resting her chin on her knees, she clamped her eyes shut as if the present reality was too much for her to acknowledge.

Heller dropped his gaze off the woman and waited for her to speak.

"Did you really mean that speech of yours?" she asked as she opened her eyes.

"Yeah, I meant it," Heller told her in a weary voice. "That doesn't mean it applies to every situation. Or every woman."

She raised her face off her knees. "You sounded bitter."

Heller appeared to mull over her words. "No. Not bitter."

"What then?"

His eyes glinted in the firelight. He drove back the memories of a terrible time when his family had been murdered, pushing the anguish back into the dark recesses of his mind. *Something I don't care to tell you about,* he thought.

She studied him. "Well, listen, cowboy, it works both ways," she said in a cold, final tone. "So I wouldn't sit around waiting for the sympathy express to come by and take you away."

Heller lifted his eyebrows and looked at her with a flint-eyed stare. But a wry twist to his lips softened his expression.

"How did you get so mean and nasty?"

She frowned.

"I only asked you to level with me in case I've gotta save both our hides again. Sympathy's the last thing I expect or need from anybody."

"How did you get so touchy?" she mimicked.

"You ought to keep your mouth shut if you don't know what the hell it is you're talking about."

"Hunh," she snorted. "The way you talk, it sounds to me

like you think you've got all the answers, mister hotshot lone-
wolf biker. And all I see is another down-and-out bike tramp
with some fancy guns. To me, that's bum—b-u-m. Nowhere
Man. You talked about these women, whoever the hell they
are, like they're to blame for something. But you show me
something. You show me what you've got," she challenged,
her voice rising in pitch to an angry whine. "You've got your
hog out there. Your open road. Your bros and your runs."

"Now who's judging who?"

"What have you got?" she repeated in a near shout.
"What have you got to really offer anybody?"

"One thing I *don't* have."

"What?"

"Windowed envelopes," he said, his lips cracking in a thin
smile.

"Oh, big deal. So you don't have any bills. Or bills you
just won't pay."

Anger surged in his gut from the tone of her bitter accu-
sation. "You're free to leave anytime you want. You're on
your own."

Fear flickered in her eyes. Her gaze dropped off Heller's
penetrating ice-blue eyes as if she was suddenly ashamed.

"I–I can't," she stammered, looking up at Heller.
"You've got to help me. Please. I can't leave. They'll kill
me."

"Who? Why?"

She hesitated. "Because . . . I saw them kill these guys."

"What guys?"

She shook her head in a gesture of frustration. "Damn
you," she cried and buried her face in her hands.

Heller let out a shallow breath in exasperation and waited.
The sound of the flames eating at the cottonwood filled the
silence.

She looked up, her face flushed. "Me and the old man had
been fighting pretty hard for a couple of months. I guess you
might know how a scene like that goes—from bad to only
worse. Well, I told him I was sick of being a biker's chick,
that I wanted something else out of life besides sex and drugs
and rock 'n' roll. He didn't like that, so I said I was leaving.

Yeah, I know.'' She looked at Heller as if to challenge him. ''Fair-weather fucking, pardon my English. But there comes a time when you have to face the music. Some do; Bo wouldn't. I'm not getting any younger, as you can see. And the crowd I left seemed to think you can stay young as long as you're irresponsible and pretend like everything's cool. I'd like to believe Mister Right is still somewhere out there.'' The intensity in her stare softened; she looked away from Heller. ''I want a family. I want a roof over my head, a real roof. I've been running since I was fourteen. I was tired of the whoring, tired of dancing in some topless joint to bring home the bread while he screwed around and stayed drunk. He couldn't accept my change of attitude, that I needed something more . . . stable. So he started beating up on me. Really bad beatings—I'd be black and blue for days. He'd just leave me alone all day and night while he was out drinking, then he'd come back to our pad crazy, stinkin' drunk or wigged out on speed. He was always threatening to kill me when he wasn't slapping me around.'' Her tone was bitterly angry. ''He'd just want to kill me. For no reason. He was just crazy. Scary crazy.''

She paused and Heller prodded, ''So what happened?''

She fished her pack of cigarettes out of her purse. Her hands shook as she lit one.

''I knew he'd gotten himself all involved with the drug scene. It was something him and Buzz Swann—that's the president of the San Angelo Sinners—had set up with some of the other clubs. Stuff and junk and big scores were all they talked about. Things seemed to go from worse straight into hell after that. Bo wasn't just using, he was selling to anyone and everyone—big time. He'd flash hundred-dollar bills around like somebody was going to be impressed, usually around some little fluffhead he was trying to hit on. He was the kind of guy who'd put two dollars of gas in his bike and hand the attendant a hundred-dollar bill just to see the look on the guy's face. It got to the point where he was bringing home these sluts and screwing them right in the next room just to piss me off. Then the son of a bitch would slap me and tell me he'd kill me if I ever messed around on him. Real sweetheart of a guy, right?''

Heller said nothing.

"One night he went out, and I followed him and Buzz and two other dudes in my girlfriend's car. I was going to catch him hitting on some chick and make a real ugly scene in front of everybody. Make sure he knew it was over. Well, it turned out he met a couple of his buyers. The guys looked college, real square. Clean-cut, slacks, the alligator shirts—that's who Bo did most of his business with. College boys using up their parents' money to keep them in snow.

"So, next thing I know Bo and this kid are arguing about the quality of the coke. The kid and his buddy against four bikers. I have to say he was gutsy but stupid for standing up to Bo and Buzz like that. But the college boy was right, and I knew it. Bo had the biggest rip-off going. He stepped on that coke every bit as bad as the kid said. I would watch him sometimes at night. He used Maalox, speed, talcum powder. He even used detergent when he didn't want to fork out the bread for speed. You'd have to snort four times what he sold you before you got any kind of real buzz; that is, if you didn't burn out your nose and your brain after three, four lines. He usually got away with it on the college kids, but not that night.''

She took a deep drag off her cigarette and blew out a long stream of smoke.

"So they killed them.''

She showed Heller a pained expression. Her brow creased with worry. "Yeah. They killed the college boys. Stabbed them both.'' Her gaze dropped. "Just left them there in their own blood to die. I read about it in the paper the next morning. One of them was a congressman's son. The father offered twenty-five thousand dollars for any information that led to an arrest and conviction.''

"How did they know you saw the killings?''

She seemed ashamed, guilt-ridden. She looked away from Heller. "I panicked and ran. They recognized the car.''

Several moments of silence passed.

Heller's forehead wrinkled up as he thought about what

she'd told him. "Well, you can bet there'll be others where those three came from. Soon. When those boys don't show up. From what you've told me, and from what I know about outlaw bikers, the drug dealing is what holds them together. That and stolen bikes and contract killings, among other things. You take the drugs away, they've got serious money problems. So what you saw and know could bring this Buzz Swann down and land him and some of the others behind bars for a long time."

"But Buzz Swann is the only one still alive that was there."

"That doesn't necessarily matter, because to the law and the general public a biker's a biker, guilty for just breathing the air and riding a bike," Heller told her. "Besides, I'm sure you've heard the biker motto—God forgives, outlaws don't."

Her solemn, downcast expression answered Heller.

"First of all, you're the only witness to two murders. Secondly, there's the drug connection. The law is aching to get anything they can on these gangs in order to crack the tight drug rings they've created. A murder rap like this could bring the whole club down. Unfortunately, the way the system is, and the way I've seen things work, it might be worse if you did turn yourself in. You'd be a clear, sitting target for the Sinners. They'd put a contract out on you. They'd get to you some way, and they wouldn't care how they did it. Your best bet right now is to keep on running. Believe me, I know."

"Christ," she sighed. "I didn't know what to do. I was scared. I ran. I guess I was hoping to just get as far away as I could. I sure didn't mean for anyone else to get involved with my problems." She looked at Heller. "Can't we just go to the cops?"

"You can. But I can't."

"What do you mean by that?" she asked, suspicious.

"I mean that wouldn't be the safest thing to do right now. People got killed back at that diner. Remember? A biker's a biker until proven innocent. Cops might just shoot first, ask questions later."

"Great." She showed Heller an imploring expression. "Will you help me?"

"I'm not going to kick you out in the cold, if that's what you mean."

"What will the cops do now?"

"There's not a lot they can do tonight because they'll be hours sorting that mess out, putting the pieces together. They'll throw up roadblocks on all the main highways and roads, put out a statewide APB with our descriptions. By morning the Rangers will be out, and there'll be a search helicopter or two. This kind of country, they'll have to use jeeps and horses, but I think we'll be all right if we don't use the paved roads. Keep to the hills until we're in the next state."

"You sound like you've been through this before."

Heller looked at her in silence and saw in her eyes a desire to pursue an inquiry. He felt annoyed, but more with himself than her. She suspected something.

"I think we should get some sleep," he said. He stood and walked away from the fire until he became a dark shape beyond the heap of rubble.

Lisa looked into the darkness that hid Heller, then turned her head and stared into the flames.

Heller walked back to the fire and dropped the heavy black bedroll on the ground, clearing away stones and adobe chips with his boots.

"It's going to get a lot colder than this tonight." Heller spread the bedroll out. "You don't mind sharing, do you?"

She twisted her head around and glanced at the sleeping bag.

"I promise I won't rape you."

She made a soft snorting sound, as if he had said something ridiculous.

Heller picked up the submachine gun. He sat down on the thick bedroll and looked at her backside. The fire burned low in front of the woman. The darkness seemed like a trap closing in on them.

"Well? I don't intend to sit here all night and freeze while you make up your mind whether or not it's safe to share the same sleeping bag. Clothed. Take it or freeze," he added in a quiet voice.

She drew on her cigarette, smoking it down to a stub. "You

go ahead. I want to sit here for a while. Maybe I'll have another cigarette. Just leave me some room."

Heller shrugged, set the Uzi down so that when he slid into the sleeping bag the subgun lay beside his head. He cupped his hands behind his head and watched the woman for a moment as she flicked the cigarette butt into the fire. She pulled another cigarette from the packet.

"Do you smoke because you're nervous?" Heller inquired. "Or does it have some deeper meaning?"

She stuck the tip of the cigarette against the flames. "I'm sexually frustrated," she cracked, her tone icy.

Heller's brow lifted.

"Forget I said that. It's just my nerves."

A thin smile crossed Heller's lips. He pulled the bedroll out from under him and spread it out like a blanket to give her space. The ground felt hard and cold against his clammy undershirt, but the bedroll trapped the heat from his body and within moments the warmth seemed to melt into his flesh. A numbness soothed his frayed nerves, relaxing his aching muscles until his eyelids felt like anvils. He couldn't remember the last time he felt so tired.

He drifted off into a deep, dreamless sleep that carried him into a black void where he felt no pain, where he was free of anguish and worry, free from the threat of violence and death. . . .

Heller's eyes opened. Dawn encroached on the night. He cursed himself for sleeping so well. For he knew men of war who had died in their sleep, choking on their own blood gushing from a slit throat or strangled by a Cong's garrote.

He sensed that something was wrong and he grabbed the Uzi and bolted upright.

Heller looked to where he'd built the fire. Wisps of smoke curled out from smoldering ash. He stood and peered into the shadows, searching the darkened crevices of the rubble.

He couldn't find the woman.

5

THE STATE TROOPER'S black-sided, white-topped cruiser was parked on the shoulder of the interstate. Directly across the four lanes on the eastbound side two more state troopers sat inside their patrol cars.

The sheriff of Apache County rolled down the window on his sleek brown patrol cruiser as he pulled off onto the Van Horn exit ramp and braked on the shoulder of the road. Both he and his deputy got out.

Dark sunglasses hid the trooper's eyes as he looked at the sheriff. "Morning, Angus. Little far from home, aren't ya?"

"Yeah, well, trouble with teletypes and radios is that bad news always travels faster than you get to it. Technology, right?"

Sheriff Angus McClan, his eyes also concealed by dark-tinted sunglasses, carved out a slice of tobacco from a brown leather pouch and popped the wad of chaw into his mouth.

The sheriff's deputy, a large, moon-faced man with a double chin, spooned the last of his chili con carne into his mouth.

"Look like you're gettin' set to direct traffic there, Buck," the square-jawed McClan said.

"Just stretching my legs. Been riding around all night trying to organize my units. I've got a real mess on my hands."

The broad-shouldered Earl "Buck" Morris wore the Special Forces insignia and an American-flag patch on the right shoulder of his black leather flight-style jacket. He put his hands on his hips, waited a moment while a battered silver Vega hatchback drove near him, then moved his right hand away from the butt of a .357 Colt Python magnum to wave the car by him.

"Heard we might have us a biker war," McClan said. "What do you know?"

"Well, looks like it's the same guy that wiped out that bunch of scum over in Bandera County. Problem is he brought some of that trash after him. Feds showed up at oh one hundred with warrants for one Jesse Heller—a vet, for chrissakes. Almost pains me to have to hunt for him. If citizens hadn't gotten killed by these punks, I'd say the guy's doing this state a big favor."

McClan turned his face away from the big trooper. "You know Bessie was cut down, don't ya?"

"I was sorry to hear that, Scotty. She'll be missed. She was a good gal." Morris spoke in a stiff, hurried manner, as if talking wasted energy he could direct toward action.

"They said the cocksuckers had them fancy Israeli subguns."

Morris nodded. "Uzis," he confirmed. "Nine-millimeter slugs chewed hell out of that diner. We found one of the Uzis at the scene of the accident. We think Heller took one with him. Feds gave me a complete description that matches the one witnesses gave me at the diner."

"Any progress?"

"Got stakeout units on every major road, north, south and west. Set a team up in an EC van in Culberson."

"You know he'll keep to the hills, don't ya?"

"Chopper team went out at oh six hundred with five jeep units. No report of any sighting yet. But I'm confident we'll get him by the day's end."

"You're not calling in to the boys at Austin?"

"No need to push the panic button. The feds want this played low key anyway. Keep the local civs at ease. They don't want the Rangers or the Guard here. Not yet. My men can handle it. How's things up in Apache?''

McClan shrugged. His sculpted face darkened with a pensive look. "Quiet, Buck. Too damned quiet for my liking." He jerked a thumb at his deputy. "But there might be a murder if Junior here don't stop eating chili for breakfast."

A thin smile cut the trooper's lips.

"I'll keep my eyes peeled, Buck, okay? You need me, call, awright?"

"Will do," Morris acknowledged. "But I think we got this one covered."

McClan nodded. He looked unconvinced by the trooper's words. "You know this boy. He used thermite to spread them bikers all over the desert in little piles of ash, Buck. He ain't just gonna throw up his hands and say, 'Come and get me.' Word I hear is the bikers want a piece of him as bad as we do. Could make for an ugly little tussle if they got the subguns."

Morris gave the sheriff a curt nod. "Keep your nose clean, Scotty. I'll be in touch if he moves your way."

McClan and the deputy got back in the cruiser and the sheriff dropped the transmission into gear and launched a long brown string of tobacco juice out the window. "Right. Later," he drawled.

The sheriff's cruiser eased away from State Trooper Colonel Earl Morris and headed slowly up the off-ramp.

A grim expression formed the trooper's face as he watched the patrol car shrink in the distance down the highway.

The first rays of morning light stabbed through scattered dark gray clouds as Jesse Heller cut through the fog-shrouded valley with his headlamp on. The high beam flickered over broken slabs of rock that rose up from the desert floor. He kept the chopper in first gear as the wheels bounced over stones and through shallow ruts. Cactus and saw-edged yucca plants reached out for him like sharp spears, forcing him to ride warily. The land stretched away from him under a murky light as sunlight tried to penetrate the clouds. The valley looked like a primeval battleground for the forces of nature, a land scorched by fire, carved by wind and water.

The footprints of the woman's moccasins had steered Heller west from the Spanish mission's debris. He knew she hadn't traveled far, for the ground beside where he'd slept had been warm and he surmised that no matter how desperate she was, only a fool would risk crossing the desert in the black of night on foot. He knew she was tough and that she was under emotional stress, but he doubted she was a fool. He was glad he had taken the keys out of the ignition before he went to sleep, something he normally didn't do.

Heller hit the throttle and the Harley shot up the side of a hill, throwing up loose sagebrush in the slipstream.

He heard the faint gush of water when he topped the rise and hand-braked the bike to a stop.

Heller snapped down the kickstand, leaned the bike over and shut off the engine. He listened to the thunderous splash of water echoing up at him as he delved into his saddlebag and pulled out his Traq 10-by-50 long-range binoculars. He climbed atop a boulder, looked through the lens, adjusted the focus.

Through the sharp, tunneled vision of the high-powered glasses, he scouted along the length of the stream that split the valley floor in a north-south direction.

He looked north, toward the cottonwood groves that flanked the stream. There he found the woman threading her way through the rocks as she advanced on the east bank. Heller watched, his mouth tight, his expression dark and intense. He saw her swing up on a cottonwood that leaned out over the water. She slipped, almost pitching into the roiling surface.

Heller lowered the binoculars. "Dumb."

Heller guided the chopper up the embankment. Cutting between creosote bushes, he rode behind the line of cottonwoods that draped out over the stream like sentinels. He braked the bike fifty feet downstream from the woman and saw her crawling out across the cottonwood as she tried to bridge the water.

Heller flipped down the kickstand and shut off the ignition. His jaw was clenched in anger as he noted the woman's gaze fixed on the three large rocks that rose up out of the stream. They were like stepping stones leading to the west bank, but Heller knew she'd never make it. He heard the tree's rotten base groan against her weight and saw the cottonwood sink several inches closer to the stream's surface. Water sprayed up into her face as she hovered over the first rock.

"Hey!"

She snapped her head sideways and flashed a startled look at Heller as he slid off the saddle.

"Don't do it," he warned. "You'll fall in. Those rocks are as slippery as ice. You might not drown, but you'll bash your head open."

"Go away."

"What the hell's the matter with you?"

She hesitated for a moment and looked with a sudden concerned expression at the moss-covered rock two feet beneath her. She wrapped her right arm halfway around the fat tree trunk.

With his arms folded over his chest, Heller watched in silence. A smug frown creased his weathered face.

She lowered her moccasins to touch the humped-up rock's slimy face and slid her arm from around the trunk.

"What do you do when you get to the other side?"

She took a tentative step onto the rock, using the palms of her hands against the tree to brace herself.

Heller drew in a breath and waited for the inevitable.

She stretched out her left leg for the middle rock and as she shoved off the tree, threw her weight forward. Water washed up over the rock beneath her feet and she slipped, crying out in alarm as she plunged into the stream.

Heller turned, pulling the .460 Weatherby rifle from its sheath, and saw her go under the surface. He jumped down the shallow bank and slid through the morass of mud and water.

Her head poked out of the water. She coughed, flailing her arms.

Heller stepped into the water and felt the stream's icy bite as water sloshed up into his face and drenched his pants. "Swim toward me!"

She stood up for a second in waist-high water, but the swift current pounded her beneath the surface again.

Heller, his right hand fisted around the root of a cottonwood, stretched out his rifle as she neared his position. She slapped the water with desperate strokes.

She cried as the current threatened to sweep her past Heller, but her fingers caught the tip of the barrel and curled around the gun sight. Her hand seemed magnetized to the barrel while the water poured over her head, pushing her under the surface.

Heller waited, staying as still as stone until she wrapped a tight grip around the barrel. The muscles in his forearms strained as he hauled the woman to him.

"Grab somethin'."

She hacked the water out of her windpipe. Her hands dug like talons into the back of Heller's undershirt. His left hand tossed the rifle up onto the bank while his right hand tightened around the root of the cottonwood. Then he grasped the root with his left hand, curled his arms and pulled them both up out of the stream.

He slipped in the mud and the woman lost her hold and fell to her knees. For a half minute she coughed and gagged, struggling to catch her breath.

Heller, his expression cut with anger and disgust, looked away from her. He picked up the high-powered Weatherby and walked to the chopper. The stream's roar filled his ears as he thrust the rifle into its sheath, a gesture that appeared to relieve some of the ire that burned in his eyes. The woman dropped back on her haunches and brushed the wet strands of hair away from her flushed face. She coughed, heaved water out of her throat, her shoulders shaking as she wiped the mud off her hands and onto Heller's jacket.

"What the hell's wrong with you, lady?"

"You're a killer," she said in a cracking voice. "I know who you are now."

Heller stood behind his chopper and peered at her. "What?"

"My purse is gone," she bitched as she fished around in her jacket pockets. "I don't have any cigarettes."

The left side of Heller's mouth crooked, his eyes glinting with sarcasm. The smell of wet leather tingled the hairs in his nose. "I'm glad you liked my jacket enough to feel free to take off with it. Wipe your muddy paws all over it."

Her breath rasped out through flared nostrils in a long, sharp sound that filled the cold silence. Water washed up over the bank behind her.

"You're the one who killed all those bikers, aren't you?"

"Lady, if I killed anybody, then it was for a damned good reason—like for taking a man's jacket."

A look of fear filled her eyes for a moment. "Funny."

"Seems like every time you get a little shook you either cut out or reach for a cigarette. Or say you're sorry, like that makes everything fine. Well, let me tell you something, it's not so fine with me." He dug into his saddlebag. Heller pulled out a lighter and a pack of Marlboro cigarettes and flipped both of them down on the ground in front of the woman. "There's your smoke."

She looked resentful for a second, but she plucked up the rumpled pack and muttered, "Thanks."

Heller saw her hand tremble as she placed a cigarette in her mouth and fire up the smoke. "Don't mention it."

The woman sucked in a long drag. Her body relaxed. She shut her eyes, relishing the feel of the smoke in her lungs as if it were some sort of narcotic. She blew out the smoke and focused a dark stare on Heller. "You did do it then. You killed all those guys like they said."

Heller's expression hardened.

The woman dropped her head, her face becoming a mask of despair. "Christ, man, isn't this just cat's ass," she sighed. "Now I've got the law and the outlaws after me." She drew on the cigarette and looked up at Heller, who stayed silent, unmoving. "Why? Why did you kill them?"

"What makes you so sure I did it?"

She exhaled a stream of smoke. "Because it's all I've been

hearing about for days. I might look stupid to you, cowboy, but I read the papers and watch the news. Jesse Heller, The lone-wolf biker, the Sinners called you. The man named Hell. Well? You're not denying it.''

Heller looked upstream. ''You want to turn yourself over to the cops, go ahead. But I've got to ride. I don't have any choice.''

The woman continued to argue, ''The Sinners were close with a lot of the Death Stalkers, you know. They'd jam together sometimes, make runs into Mexico. The talk I heard is that Buzz Swann and his boys want the dude who snuffed out the Stalkers. That was just two days ago, when I was at their clubhouse with Bo. They have enough firepower to field an army. Are you listening to me?''

Heller turned his head and faced the woman.

''They're riding out. They're coming after you,'' she said. She let out a breath, shook her head. ''Now they'll really have their chance to kill two birds.''

''Let 'em ride. They're not alone, lady.''

''Stop calling me lady. I've got a name. It's Lisa.'' She rose to her feet, her knees cracking as she stood, and stuffed the lighter and pack of Marlboros into the jacket pocket. ''As far as choices go, I guess I don't have any either,'' she declared, sounding somber all of a sudden. ''I lost my head last night. I thought maybe you would . . . that you were . . .''

''Do I look like some kind of lunatic to you? Do lunatics pull people out of flooded streams?''

She searched his level gaze. She stayed silent for a long moment, then flicked the cigarette stub away from her. ''I don't know. But I guess I should, since crazy nuts are all I've ever been around and you're not like them.''

Heller hopped on the chopper and grasped the handlebars. ''I gotta make tracks. You comin'?''

''Why did you kill them?''

Heller looked toward the barren hills. He felt the wetness of his clothes sinking into his skin. Anguish clawed at his guts like a grappling iron.

''They killed my family. They raped and murdered the woman I would've married.'' He looked at the woman. His

eyes glittered through slitted lids. He swallowed and a lump
went down his throat like a stone to lodge in his chest. "After
all the shit, after all the blood over there, all the men I watched
die—all I wanted was to get back to something I could call
my own to some sanity. Like you, maybe all I wanted was a
real roof over my head and a family I could come home to
every night, know that they were there for me." Heller swallowed again. "But I was cheated. They paid, but maybe I'm
not really sure now, maybe I've lost more by killing them
than I gained. It's a helluva thing to kill a man. It's an insanity. It's something you can't really see when you're going
through it."

She dropped her stare from Heller. "I'm sorry."

Heller snapped back the kick stand. "Don't be. It's over."
He jumped down on the kick starter and the Harley revved to
life. He waited while Lisa climbed onto the buddy seat. She
took the black helmet from his saddlebag, pushed it down
over her hair and fastened on the chin strap.

They sat in silence for a moment. Jesse Heller let the grief
of the memory slowly fade from his mind.

"Let's go," she urged. "We've got to make tracks."

He stamped down on the gearshift, feeling the woman's
eyes on the back of his head. He turned his head slightly as
she wrapped her arms around his midsection.

She leaned up in the seat. "Hey."

Heller cocked his head.

"Thanks for pulling my dumb ass out of there."

Heller faced front. He let the clutch out and pulled away
from the muddy bank. "I haven't pulled anybody out of
anything yet."

The big black iron beast lurched up the rocky slope as
thunder rumbled down from the hills and rolled across the
dark valley sky.

The more Buzz Swann learned about women, the better he
liked his '48 Panhead. He'd lost count of how many old ladies he'd packed with over his thirteen years as an outlaw
biker—four of which he'd spent in Leavenworth for assault
with a deadly weapon. His time behind the wall had been for

beating an off-duty cop into a bloody, simpering pulp with brass knuckles. A bum rap to Buzz Swann.

But Buzz Swann's run-ins with the Man had been mere skirmishes when he recalled the grief women had caused him. He couldn't even count the days and nights of endless mental and emotional anguish that had sent him into fits of rage over women.

It embarrassed Buzz Swann only a little to remember how many times his crotch had been ravaged by the clap until he'd been ready to castrate himself to relieve the pain. But it hurt him a lot to think about the good romps he'd missed with the young chicks who'd stomped out the door when he'd parked his sled in the bedroom or left a disassembled crankcase or a manifold gasket in a pool of oil on the sheets. Memories tended to bring out the bitterness in him. Visions of past old ladies nagging about playing second fiddle to a bike usually sent Buzz Swann's blood pressure straight into his brain until he felt his heart throbbing in his ears like the beat of a war drum.

The kickstand of his dark-blue-painted Panhead rested on a solid four-inch cinder block, the oil draining down into a bowl. Swann stared at the oil. He didn't like the dark, gummy viscosity and he wished he had changed the oil a thousand miles ago like he normally would have if it hadn't been for a run down to Los Herreras. Now he was glad that he had at least stripped down the carburetor and changed the plugs the night before last.

Wrenches, sockets, an impact screwdriver, a timing light, a compression gauge, a soldering iron, a degree wheel and a vacuum gauge were spread out neatly on a spotless black canvas sheet. Swann's arm muscles rippled beneath an array of tattoos as he wiped the grease off his hands with a white rag, before he slipped off the chrome-plated primary outer cover and set it down gently on the canvas sheet. He couldn't think of anything else to do right then—he'd cleaned the oil pump filter, adjusted the drive chain and brakes, adjusted the clutch and tappets, greased the tachometer drive unit, lubricated the valves with lead—so he decided he'd polish the chrome cover.

"Buzz."

He pushed himself up off his rump and squatted on his haunches, oblivious to the sound of the female voice. He waited for the final few drops of oil to drain.

"Hey. Asshole."

Buzz Swann rose to his full five foot seven inches of height. A look of annoyance cocked the left side of his square, suntanned face. His blue denim Levi's were clean except for the dark splotches of ingrained grease. Sweat soiled his sleeveless green undershirt. HARLEY-DAVIDSON was printed on it in white letters over a death's-head with a black eye patch on the right eye socket. A spider web spread out from the skull and its teeth clutched a logo that read TIL DEATH DO US PART. Swann wore a thin blond beard and a handlebar mustache that curled and drooped symmetrically down the sides of his mouth.

"Figured that would get your attention."

An oil filter plunked in the dirt beside Swann as he turned toward the mobile trailer home.

"You lost your mind, woman?" Swann rasped as he picked up the filter. "Throwing a goddamned brand-new filter around like that. What the hell's wrong with you?"

A big-breasted woman with disheveled ash-blond hair poked her head through the trailer's doorway. The dark circles under her eyes outlined her sunken gaze, testifying to a hangover or lack of sleep, or both. Her hand fisted around the inside doorknob, keeping the door hanging askew on its rusty bottom hinge. A baby cried from inside the trailer.

"You want to eat or not? The eggs are almost done. You know, if you spent as much time with me and the baby as you do with that bike I wouldn't have to sound like such a whiny bitch all the time."

Swann's angry expression softened, but his tone was grudging as he told her, "I'll be there in a few minutes. They said it's gonna rain."

"Big deal." She scowled and slammed the door shut.

"Hell, I can't just leave parts everywhere, damn you!"

The baby's wailing pierced through the trailer's sides.

"Shut up!" Swann heard the woman yell.

A mangy black Labrador lifted its head from in back of the trailer. Its dark glassy eyes stared up at Swann. Flies buzzed around the dog's head where Swann had accidentally shot the Labrador's left ear off the previous New Year's Eve.

"Women, huh, boy?" he muttered to the dog. "Sometimes they just make me want to kick ass."

The trailer door opened and the baby's squalling seemed to blast out across the barren, trash-littered yard.

Anger flared in Swann's blue eyes. He shot his gaze toward his old lady and he braced himself for a stormy confrontation.

"Your arm-breaker—I believe you call him your enforcer—called," she yelled over the child's wailing.

"When?"

"Twenty minutes ago."

"Why didn't you say something?"

"I did," she squawked. "You either didn't hear me or you just ignored me. As usual."

"What did he want?"

"How should I know?"

Swann shook his head and shot a disgusted look at the woman.

"It's hard to get your attention, you know. You've been sitting out here since four o'clock in the morning. You look like you're getting ready to dip your wick into that bike." She started to close the door but thrust it back open. "Maybe you should. It might be the perfect fit."

The Labrador flinched as she banged the door shut.

"Shut up, please," the woman cried.

"Madness. Fuckin' madness," Swann growled, stooping over his tools and reaching for the chrome cover. But he froze as the sound of a chopper reached his ears. He turned his head in the direction of the engine noise and saw a plume of dust trailing Smoky as the Nazi-helmeted Sinner roared up the dirt drive.

Swann stood. His face tightened with a look of dark curiosity.

Smoky braked the chopper in front of the chapter president and shut off the ignition. Dust settled behind the outlaw.

Swann knew something was wrong because of the crazed expression on Smoky's face. He'd seen the look on the outlaw before. "What's the matter? Where's Bo?"

A film of dust looked as if it had been carefully sprinkled on Smoky's beard and over his long, oily hair. The lanky biker's gaze widened. The excitement seemed to clear away some of the bloodshot red in his eyes. "Bo told me to head back. He thinks he's got that lone-wolf dude that snuffed Buddy Silvers. They were runnin' west—the dude and Bo's old lady."

"Slow down. Wait a minute. I hope you're not telling me something got screwed up."

"Uh-uh. Called Bugger about an hour ago. Told him the gig. Said he'd call—maybe he already has, I don't know, but he wants a meeting. Quick like." Smoky's muscles visibly tensed, the veins on his forehead throbbing. "Shit, Buzz, I'm trying to tell ya we can get the dude that wasted Silvers and Burton's boys."

Swann peered at Smoky. He felt his heart speed up. "How do you know it was him?"

"Some old geezer at a gas stop gave us the lowdown. Big black Harley. Big guns. Busted-up face. Same dude Slinky and them said burned down the house."

"Bo went after him? The bitch too?"

Smoky nodded. His breath spurted through his nose.

Buzz Swann looked lost in thought for a moment. A dark expression clouded his face. "Okay. No time to rap now. You get over to Bugger's. Round up thirty bros, meet me at the clubhouse in an hour. First I gotta get my bike back together."

"We ridin' out? Goin' after him?"

Swann wheeled and bent over his tools. "You bet your white ass."

Smoky let out a harsh laugh as he hopped down on the kick starter. "Hot fuckin' damn. See you there!" he called, his voice washed out by a roaring engine burst as he rolled the blue Panhead around and patched out of the dirt drive on a peal of thunder. Dust cloaked his departure.

Swann hurried to put the primary outer cover back on. His hands worked frantically.

If it was true, and he had no reason to doubt Smoky's word, then they would be on a run within hours. The run of a lifetime.

A grim smile stretched Swann's lips as he thought about the man they called Hell, about the stories of his exploits that had circulated through different clubhouses. The dude had wasted a lot of class outlaw brothers in the name of vengeance. No outlaw worth his colors would just let the lone wolf ride. Swann wanted some vengeance of his own. He wanted to make Heller an example of what would happen to any redneck or citizen who thought he could take the law into his own hands.

There was no time to waste.

But a look of regret flashed through his gaze as he stared at his beautifully restored Panhead, his pride and joy, which had been re-created through hours of tireless labor. He almost hated to take her out on the road, especially on what he knew would be a blood run.

Now, though, Swann felt the excitement burn in his blood. He anticipated one hellstorming run.

It had been awhile since he'd been in a good fight.

And old ladies didn't count.

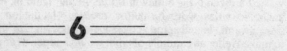

6

*T*HE BOTTLE OF Jim Beam rolled off the couch and thudded on the tan carpet. Light brown liquor sloshed out of the bottle's nose, soaking into the edges of three *Playboy* magazines.

Wes Garrett pulled his face up off the pillow and looked down at the bottle through bloodshot, bleary eyes. He swung his left arm down and grasped the bottle, setting it upright. He smelled the sweat on himself, a harsh, biting odor that pinched through his nostrils and pierced like ammonia into his brain. He cursed. His limbs felt as heavy as lead. His white dress shirt and black slacks stuck to his clammy skin as if they were pasted on with a sticky glue, as if he'd been in a sauna for two days instead of in his apartment, drinking and brooding. His swollen bladder made him wonder when he'd last relieved himself.

Garrett ran the palms of his hands over the thick black-and-gray stubble along his square jaw and slicked the sweat back into his gray hair.

A buzzing sound slowly penetrated the pounding pain in his head.

He glanced around the apartment toward the drapes where a crack of light spilled into the room. From what he could last remember, his place looked like either a combat zone, or a small Kansas town after a twister. He flicked on the light switch on the lamp beside the couch and squinted into the brightness. He found his suspicion confirmed.

Burger King food wrappers, girlie magazines, beer cans and Coca-Cola cans littered the apartment floor. The sight caused Garrett to emit another moan. The thought of having to clean up the disaster suddenly made him wish for a good stiff belt of Jim boy.

Garrett stood, the bones in his knees and feet cracking as he rose to his six feet two inches of height. He ambled across the room, kicking through a sea of crumpled Budweiser cans before he turned into the kitchen. He snatched up the phone receiver that dangled down the wall on its coiled yellow cord and slammed it into the hookup.

He went to the faucet, leaned his head into the sink and twisted on the cold-water knob. Water spumed out of the nozzle, matted his hair to his head, helping to revive his senses. He lifted his head and banged the back of his skull on the spout. Cursing he turned off the water.

He smoothed back his hair, throwing drops of water on the white face of the refrigerator door. Water streaked down the door like skinny, colorless snakes.

It had been a long time since he'd felt so wrung out, so physically and emotionally drained.

Garrett couldn't even remember what he'd done except drink himself into a stupor the past two days. This after the tongue-lashing Captain Allison had dealt him and his partner for the "insubordinate way" they'd handled the Death Stalker stakeout. It was, according to the captain, the "biggest fiasco and embarrassment" the Dallas Police Department had ever been made to suffer.

But at the moment Garrett didn't give a damn about anything. Perhaps, he thought gloomily, he'd been a cop too long, and the years of seeing the ruins people made of their lives had finally made him apathetic. But he wasn't quite sure if it was the booze that helped him feel so indifferent, or if it was the memories of the hell he'd made out of his own life. The bottle had more than once threatened to end his police career. After two marriages, it had become like a shadowy killer following him around, something he dreaded but found himself unable to confront.

He opened the refrigerator door and found a six-pack of beer. He reached for it, but stopped when he heard the knock on his apartment door.

He shoved the refrigerator door shut, rattling the dishes in the cabinets. He moved out of the kitchen, kicked into an empty beer can and sent it clattering across the hallway. He cursed.

Garrett looked through the peephole and felt his heart skip a beat. He stood unmoving for a moment, deciding what to do. His hand trembled as he unlocked and opened the door. He stood in silence for a stretched second as he locked gazes with Captain Allison.

"Well, Captain, to what do I owe the pleasure? Is this an official or an unofficial visit?"

Garrett's voice was gravelly. He cleared away the phlegm in his throat.

"Mind if I come in for a minute, Wes?"

Garrett was stunned but masked his surprise with an expression of cold indifference. It had been years since Allison had used his first name, perhaps as long ago as when they'd both been patrolmen. They had been friends for a brief time before Allison quickly moved up in rank and forgot who his friends were.

Garrett's shoulders sagged. He suddenly felt very tired.

"What's the matter?" Garrett said as he turned away. "Didn't you chew off enough ass the other day?"

Allison was silent for a moment. He seemed uncertain about something and looked regretful.

Garrett reached into his shirt pocket and brought out a rumpled pack of cigarettes. "You want a drink?" he asked, a bitter edge to his voice. He flicked out a cigarette, stuck the ruffle-edged smoke in his mouth. "I got about a half dozen slices of processed cheese if you're hungry." He struck a match and fired up the smoke.

Allison stepped into the apartment. He stood six and a half feet tall in his brown leather cowboy boots. He wore light brown slacks and a tan pullover sweater that outlined a long, lean, muscular physique.

"Wes, I'm going to get right to the point."

"You always had a direct way about you, Captain. Even when we were drinking buddies. You do remember the good old days, don't you?" Garrett drew on his cigarette. The ice he felt in his gut seemed to melt away as he pulled the smoke deep into his lungs.

Allison's dark eyes looked over the apartment before he rested a somber gaze on Garrett. "I want you to take a little time off."

"I've already had two days off. At the chief's request. Or have you forgotten our little meeting down at the city council already?"

Allison's attention shifted to the bottle in front of the couch. "You've had the phone off the hook. Your partner said you either weren't here or you wouldn't answer the door."

"Look, Captain, I'm a little tired, that's all."

"I'm afraid it's a lot more than just being tired or frustrated, Wes. You're not ready to come back to work. Christ, I could smell this place from out in the street."

Garrett stared at Allison. He looked for the humor in the captain's eyes but didn't find it.

"And all I have to do is take one look around here, and I can tell that maybe I've got a cop who's just about ready to come apart. A cop on the edge. This department doesn't need a walking time bomb.

"That stakeout of yours was a complete disaster. The city cannot and will not finance revenge hunts. The whole thing was one big waste of time and money. You violated departmental procedure by not reporting in, then going off after this Heller on your own. You put the lives of the men under you in unnecessary danger. The reports you filled out were sloppy and incomplete. Your attitude is now clearly hostile and belligerent. And certain members of your team stated in their reports that you seemed like a man possessed with having to bring Heller in."

"Dudley?" Garrett asked, a look of incredulous anger in his eyes.

"No," Allison shot back, his tone flat and final.

"I'm suspended, is that what you're saying, Captain?"

"You've been a cop for eighteen years, Garrett." Allison faltered for a moment. "I think we were even friends once."

"Before you moved on to bigger and better things. Forgot just who your friends were."

"Things happen, Wes. Life takes . . . certain directions. You've had some damned good moments, but I've also looked the other way for you more than once—because we were once friends. But I can't cover for you anymore. I tried to hang in there with you, make some allowances when both your marriages fell apart. At least then I could get along with you because I saw a dedicated cop who was making a sincere effort."

"Would it have made any difference if I'd brought Heller in?"

"Maybe. Maybe not," Allison said. "But notice that you just said 'I.' "

"He made me look bad, Captain. Made me feel like I couldn't do my job."

"See, Garrett? That's what I'm talking about. I don't think you're seeing your job, your role as a law-enforcement officer as a service to the community. You're seeking personal glory, Garrett. And if that's what it's come down to, then as far as I'm concerned. you're through as a cop."

Garrett let the cigarette smoke stream out of his nostrils. He worked his jaw. The veins in his temples pulsed.

"So, yes, you're suspended. Unofficially at this time until further notice, until I decide if any further disciplinary action is necessary."

Garrett dropped his stare off Allison and walked to the far corner of the room. He felt like someone had just told him he was dying of cancer. He drew on the cigarette.

"Is that all? *Captain.*"

Allison let the breath rasp sharply out of his nose. "For now. Come see me in my office Monday morning. The chief will be there with a review board. I'm sorry about all of this, Wes.''

Garrett heard the door open and close, but it was a sound that seemed to come from miles away as he retreated into anger and bitter resentment. He let the cigarette drop from his lip and ground out the butt on the carpet. He looked at the bookcase, letting his stare rest on the portrait of himself in his high school football uniform. The pigskin was tucked under his left arm, his right arm extended for a forearm shiver. He saw an eighteen-year-old kid with a smooth, handsome face and a cocky glint in his eyes. Times were simple then, he thought, when all he had to think about was scoring the next touchdown, his only worry his girlfriend. Allison was right. Life had a way of changing. For Garrett, the metamorphosis had grown out of broken dreams, lost hope. It had been twenty years since he'd made all-American as a running back at Stonewall Jackson High School. Twenty years since he'd had his last taste of glory. It had seemed downhill from there. A steep downhill slide on bared asshole.

Garrett's heart felt heavy in his chest.

Heller was out there somewhere. Running wild like a hungry animal. Garrett recalled their encounter at the diner. He'd had his chance then to stop the lone-wolf biker, but he'd blown it. Deep inside he sympathized with Jesse Heller's plight, with his burning desire to see justice prevail in a system that appeared to be going to shit.

But Garrett knew Jesse Heller had to be stopped. Wars claimed the innocent as well as the guilty. But, Garrett wondered, what price should a man be willing to pay, what sacrifice should be made in order to insure a better world? Had Heller's war made anything better? Garrett pondered.

He strode across the room and into the kitchen. He picked up the phone and dialed the precinct.

''Joe. Yeah, hi, it's Wes. Anything come over the teletype on Jesse Heller? What's that?''

Garrett's expression darkened. His eyelids narrowed over an intense gaze and his lips hinted at a wolfish smile.

Rage simmered in Buzz Swann's eyes.

"When?"

"Yesterday evening. All three of them bought it, Buzz. Over the high side for Bo."

Buzz Swann just stared at his sergeant-at-arms, Bugger Jensen, as if his mind could not register the news of the violent deaths of three of their outlaw brothers.

The amassed roar of chopper engines seemed to shake the hardwood floor beneath Swann's feet as outlaws parked on the lawn outside the split-level home.

"The Man's gonna come down hard on us, Buzz, I'm tellin' ya. Bo and Sniddy snuffed a coupla citizens," Jensen informed him. "It was dumb, yeah, to shoot up that diner. But if Bo was pumped full of speed—well, shit, he goes crazy when he gets that stuff in him.

"Sniddy's old lady got hassled this morning at four. Son-of-a-bitchin' pig flat out told her there wasn't enough of Sniddy left to scrape up on a spatula, like he was proud. She said she even heard someone snickering in the background, wanted to know if she would identify the remains."

Swann looked away from the beefy, bearded biker and focused a hard-eyed gaze on the armament that was piled along the far wall. He looked at the Uzis, the M-16s, the Colt .45s and magnum revolvers, the Mossberg and Remington pump shotguns. He wondered how much lead they could all chew Heller up with before he died.

"This lone-wolf motherfucker's gotta be snuffed," Jensen said. He had a deep voice that seemed to rise up out of his barrel chest like a peal of thunder. He wore dark sunglasses; his jaw jutted out away from the rest of his face as if someone had taken a sledgehammer and bashed his face in; scar tissue ran down his left cheek. "The bros are gettin' real uptight about this crazy dude."

"Don't get nervous, Bugger," Swann said. "We'll take care of him. He's only one man."

The sound of heavy bike boots clomping up the wooden stoop snared Swann's attention. Outlaws pushed into the living room. Within moments the thirty chosen Sinners, all dressed in full colors, stood in grim silence before Swann.

Someone let out a soft whistle at the sight of the firepower.

"Okay, listen up," Jensen started.

The harsh smell of sweat and marijuana smoke filled the room. A biker pitched a beer can out of the door. Dark sunglasses hid two dozen pairs of eyes. The anger and hostility seemed like a palpable force in the room as the outlaws bunched together like pigs in a sty.

"Most of you already know why this run's happenin'," Jensen said.

Swann leaned back into the staircase railing and folded his arms over his chest. He looked over the faces of some of his men—Turd, Chaos, Cheese Nuts, Wing Ding, Flathead, the squat, fat twin brothers, Lobo and Bobo.

Buzz Swann had started the Sinners outlaw motorcycle club two years after his discharge from the Army. He knew Jensen, Mad Mike and Pisser from his Vietnam War days when they'd served in the same platoon. Together, following the war, they'd ridden through some tough, ugly times. They had come back to the World, to a society that seemed to fear every veteran as some psychopathic killing machine. There was no work for them, except for menial labor—car-wash jobs or janitorial work. Destitution had brought them together. Big, powerful bikes and the open road, beer, loose women and easy money made from drug-dealing and selling stolen bike parts—these things had bonded them through post-Nam.

But there was something else that held them together, a feeling that went deep into each of them and let them hold their heads high when everything else went to hell. It was a feeling greater than just friendship—a brotherhood of men who shared the love of the freedom of biker law. The colors made them somebody, made the society that cast them off as losers take notice.

The thirty men gathered in front of Swann were all original members, and he knew he could trust and depend on every single one of them. They'd all shown real class in the past.

"We got us an asshole out there that snuffed Bo, Sniddy and Igor last night," Jensen continued. "The same asshole that took out the Death Stalkers and Burton's chapter. We're going after that dude. That's why you're here." Jensen paused. "All that hardware you see is gonna be put to use, or don't bother touchin' it. Everyone here's been trained how to use it. But on dummy targets. Now, what I'm tellin' ya is that we might have to go up against the Man before we get to the asshole. Anyone who can't handle the scene is free to ride."

A second of silence followed the grim warning. No one moved, for everyone knew that to leave the room at that moment meant being disregarded by the club—a painful, humiliating ritual in which an outlaw would have his club tattoos cut off his flesh in front of the whole club and which could also result in a death sentence.

"When we ride outa here," Swann said, "we go quiet. Sheathe every piece. We run together, but do the speed limit. No yelling and hollering and blowing minds. Bugger's coming behind us with another twenty men thirty minutes after we leave. Case there's trouble. Case we're stopped by the pigs."

"Go outa your way to keep from tanglin' with the Man," Jensen said.

"What if the pigs go outa their way to hassle us?" Turd asked. He was a beer-bellied biker with no visible neck and an oval-shaped head that rested like a bowling ball on his shoulders.

"Pigs force a play—burn 'em. This ain't no beer run. This is a blood run," Swann told them. "And I mean to get this son of a bitch. Bo, Sniddy and Igor were class bros all the way. Everyone here loved them. Nobody's ever fucked with us like this. We owe it to them."

"Heard the dude's got Bo's old lady," Chaos called out. He was a biker with bushy black hair that stuck out in long, oily spikes.

"I don't know what the whole story on that is, but don't kill her if you can help it. She split to tell the pigs about the college boys. Y'all know about that scene. So I need to know what she said, and to who. Any more questions?"

"Shit, this dude's as good as dead, Buzz," Lobo said.

Swann raked his gaze over the outlaws. He drew in a deep breath. Sweat formed on his brow. It was getting hot and stuffy in the room. He wondered why he suddenly didn't feel as confident as he knew he should.

"Man, this is fuckin' nuts," Mad Mike, a biker with a shaved head, said in a low, awestruck tone. He smiled. His gaze widened. "Just like back in the fuckin' jungle, babe."

Mad Mike had busted a lot of heads for Swann. He had contracted himself out to kill off some of the drug competitors who had cut in on Sinner turf. It was rumored that Mad Mike liked to chain-whip his victims to death, though no one had ever seen him take a mark out. "You gotta love it, mothas."

Swann waited for any other comments. He sensed the tension in the room.

"Done then," Swann said. The number 13 was tattooed on the back of the clenched left fist he raised. "For our dead bros," Swann said.

The thirty Sinners lifted balled left fists.

"FOR OUR BROTHERS!"

Swann felt a ball of sweat trickle down his forehead and burn into his eye. "The devil help whoever gets in our way."

Garrett braked the brown Ford in front of the wood-and-stucco ranch-style house.

He had dressed in tan trousers and a light brown tweed sports jacket and had shaved and showered. But his eyes were still glassy from the effects of two days of hard, nonstop drinking. He was gaunt and pale from having gone three days without food, but he felt his heart beat with hope and excitement. The news that Jesse Heller had been spotted in the southwest part of the state made him forget how bad he felt.

Garrett swung open the car door and stepped out into the street. He experienced a stab of trepidation, fearing that his partner might not share his enthusiasm after their first encounter with the renegade bounty hunter.

The hard rubber soles of Garrett's black shoes rapped over the concrete walk. He stopped under the awning in front of the glass door to Dudley's house. His reflection on the glass shadowed back at him, a ghostly silhouette against the dim

light in the hallway corridor. Garrett stared at his tired-look-
ing, haggard face for a moment. A little girl's voice broke
his gaze.

"Daddy. Daddy, it's Uncle Wes."

Dudley's six-year-old daughter scurried down the hall. Her
pink dress fluttered behind her. Her blond pigtails bounced
off her white blouse. A sad smile creased Garrett's lips. But
then he saw the massive shape of his six-foot-six-inch-tall,
two-hundred-and-sixty pound partner step into the hallway
and lumber toward him. The smile faded from Garrett's lips.

"Wes. Where the h— Where you been?" Dudley swung
the door open. "Come on in. Hell, your phone's been off the
hook. I almost broke your door down yesterday I been so
worried." Dudley paused. He studied Garrett's bleary eyes,
the sagging mouth line, the glassy stare. "Christ, Wes, you
look like hell. I should've figured. You been hitting it hard,
haven't ya? And with Allison looking to nail you that's the
last thing you need."

"I've already seen Allison."

Dudley's eyebrows arched. "And?" he prodded.

"I'm suspended. Unofficially, that is."

Dudley exhaled a long breath. "I was afraid of something
like that."

"I'm going after Heller."

Dudley's eyes narrowed. "What? Oh, come on,
Wes. . . ."

"They've got him on the run. They think somewhere near
Culberson County."

"Wes, let it go, for God sakes. We turned it over to the
FBI. Let the feds handle it."

Garrett shook his head. He opened his mouth to speak, but
Dudley's little girl walked in from the hall and he froze.

Dudley turned his attention to his daughter. "Come here,
baby," he said as he bent and picked the girl up in his arms.
"Say hi to Uncle Wes."

"Are you taking Daddy to work?" She hooked a finger in
her mouth and showed Garrett blue eyes that seemed to spar-
kle with sunshine.

Garrett felt embarrassed. He tried to smile but lost the smile to a feeling of foolishness.

"Wes? Who's here?"

Dudley looked away from Garrett. "It's Wes, honey."

"Is everything all right?" she called from the next room. "With Wes, I mean?"

"How are you, Sheila?" Garrett said.

"Dud's been worried sick about you, Wes. Where have you been? You'll have to excuse me for not coming out, but I'm getting dressed. We're late for church. Your partner can't seem to get out of bed on his days off."

Garrett looked flustered. "Look, I'll talk to you some other time."

"Wait a minute." Dudley lowered his daughter to the hallway floor. He kissed her on the forehead. "Go tell Mommy I'll be there in a minute."

She spun and ran down the hall. "Little Sue'll be seven next week," he said as he watched his daughter disappear through the archway. He smiled.

"Listen, Dud. I'm going to be there when they take Heller. I'd rather be the one to do it, but if I can't . . . You coming with me?"

Dudley shrugged his shoulders. He held his hands out. "You realize what you're asking me? I've got a family to feed, Wes. I've got to hold on to my job. I can't just take off, running all over the country. Forget Heller. He's not our problem anymore."

The left side of Garrett's face twisted. "So, is that the way it's going to be? I'm disappointed in you, Dud. We've been partners and friends for twelve years. We've been up against a lot uglier jams than this Heller guy could ever push us into."

"Why do you want him so bad?"

"My badge is on the line, Dud. Unlike you, I don't have a family. I got two people I brought into this world and raised who'd like to shit all over the very ground I walk on. I married the first piece of ass I ever got because I was too young to know any better," Garrett said in a harsh whisper. "The second bitch also decided that a cop's salary just couldn't keep her in the finer things of life, and when she wasn't drinking away my money she was fucking half the guys in town. So it's my job, Dud. That's what it all comes down to. That's all I've got left. I'd hoped to Christ you of all people would've understood that.''

"Okay, okay, easy. Keep your voice down. I'm going to church right now. Can I meet you somewhere in about two hours?''

"You coming with me? After Heller?''

"What am I supposed to tell Sheila?''

"Easy—tell her the truth.''

Dudley nodded. A look of resignation formed on his features.

"I'll be at the Whisky River. Will I see you there?''

Dudley nodded.

Garrett turned and opened the door. He left Dudley standing in the hallway by himself.

The big cop jammed his hands into his pants pockets. He shook his head softly.

"Dud," his wife called. "Wes leave?''

"Yeah. He's gone.''

"Is he all right?''

Dudley watched his partner through the door glass as Garrett opened the front door of the Ford, slid in and slammed the door shut.

"No," Dudley muttered. "He's not.''

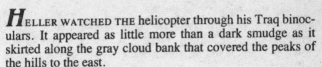

7

*H*ELLER WATCHED THE helicopter through his Traq binoculars. It appeared as little more than a dark smudge as it skirted along the gray cloud bank that covered the peaks of the hills to the east.

"What is it? What do you see?"

Heller stayed silent for a moment before he answered, "A copter. They're out there looking for us. One reason why I thought we should wait up here for a while. If there was any pursuit behind us, I was hoping they might head on past."

"Do you think they'll find us?"

Heller lowered the binoculars and stared out at the rugged plateau that stretched away from the hill. "I'm not sure. But they're headed north like they know something."

"I thought north was the way you wanted to go."

Heller looked pensive. "Was."

"What do you mean by that?"

"Well, the thing is, nobody's seen us yet except the driver of that semi back on the interstate. I'm thinking maybe we should head east, backtrack. They expect us to keep heading west, or maybe into Mexico." He heard the woman sigh, faced her, saw an expression of weary pain on her face. "What's the matter with you?"

"Nothing."

"What's wrong?"

She stared at Heller for a moment. "Do you actually believe you can get away after what you did?"

Heller turned away from her and looked back into the binoculars. He looked to where his chopper lay hidden by brush in the gorge below him, then scouted the desolate terrain. "If you really want to know the truth—no, I didn't plan on getting away with it." He took the glasses away from his eyes. "But that doesn't mean I can't."

"What if it comes down to you having to shoot it out with some cops?"

"It won't."

"But it could."

"It won't," he said adamantly. "I never meant for any innocent party to get hurt."

"But they have."

Heller worked his jaw, ignoring her for a second. "We're going to stay here tonight. We'll be safe. There's got to be a town or a service station somewhere on the other side of those hills."

"Somewhere?"

"Well, we're going to take a ride and find out. I've got to call somebody."

"Who? Your wife?"

Heller swung his head and fixed a sharp stare on her.

"I'm sorry," she blurted. "I forgot. I'm sorry."

Heller let the breath rasp out his nose. He stood up from behind the boulder. Anger smoldered in his gaze as he looked away from the woman.

"Do you think it might be easier if you ditched the bike?"

A bitter half smile formed on his lips. She sounded exasperated all of a sudden. "You gotta be kidding." He moved down the side of the hill, rocks sliding away from beneath his boots. "Come on. It's too late now to be grabbing at straws."

A long line of dust folded in the chopper's wake as it wound down the narrow dirt trail that spined through the steep gorge. The sheer walls of rock stretched two hundred feet high, seeming to poke straight into the gray clouds that scudded overhead.

Heller followed the path out of the gorge and began threading his way across a rolling plain. An endless sea of sagebrush and creosote bushes flanked the couple. The woman kept her arms wrapped tightly around Heller as the bike's wheels jarred now and again through ruts and threatened to topple them both into waiting coats of prickly cactus.

The wind swept across the barren plain with a low, mournful sound that rustled through the brush. Indeed, the breeze appeared to breathe tumbleweed in front of the chopper, as if ghosts of the Apache Indians who once made the Guadalupe Range their domain had come down from the caves that laced the mountainside to greet Heller and the woman.

Heller looked east and saw the gypsum salt flats that humped up out of the plain and rolled in white waves toward isolated mountain chains. Patches of blue sky broke through the cloud banks.

Heller felt the woman tap his shoulder. He faced front, braked the chopper and downshifted to a halt. He sat utterly still for long moments. Cold anger knotted his gut.

A look of revulsion showed on the woman's face as she peered over Heller's shoulder.

The mule deer's black eyes stared up at them as if beseeching them. Its tongue lolled from the corner of its mouth. The antlers of the once-powerful buck were chipped, cracked—but not from a duel with a rival male. A pool of blood stretched away from behind the buck, leading to the carcasses of a doe and two fawns.

What had once been sleek-looking muscular animals with smooth brown fur were now lumps covered in a slick red morass of blood. Dozens of bullet holes stitched the length of their bodies. Flies swarmed over the gory wounds. A nine-inch scorpion crabbed out of the brush, as if drawn to death like a magnet. It parted the crimson puddle with its pincers and curved tail to close in on one of the fawns.

Jesse Heller felt the sorrow stab into him like a knife. It was one thing to kill an animal for food, or to use its hide to combat the elements. But he found senseless acts of slaughter for the sheer, perverse thrill of killing to be something close to an abomination. Whoever had butchered the deer had used an automatic or semi-automatic weapon. This Heller judged by the pattern of shots across the carcasses.

"What kind of idiot does something like that?"

Heller looked at the set of tire tracks. They showed thick treads in the loose soil. Jeep tracks.

He drew a deep breath, slipped the bike into gear and let out the clutch. He rolled past the inert forms.

Lisa looked back at the mutilated remains, her mouth downturned by a look of bitter anguish.

Dust settled over the dead deer.

A lone black buzzard dipped down from the sky as the sound of the Harley's snarling engine trailed across the desert floor.

They found the jeep two miles down the trail.

The back end of the black Renegade jeep was lifted up on a jack and blocked the path, forcing Heller to slow down.

The noise of the chopper's growling engine alerted three men.

A big potbellied man stepped from around the front of the jeep, cradling an M-16. He wore a sheepskin coat, Levi's blue jeans and scuffed tan hiking boots. The insides of the man's shoe heels were worn down and made his knees buckle in slightly.

As Heller closed to within thirty feet of the jeep, the two men by the jack looked up.

The man who had taken the spare tire out of the jeep now set the tire down and leaned it against the fender. He was a short, stocky man with a beak-shaped face that gave him the appearance of a buzzard. A mane of snow-white hair was combed back away from his high forehead and reached the shoulders of his brown leather jacket. The third man, squatted beside the exposed wheel rim, wore a crew cut that stuck up two inches off a bullet-shaped head.

Heller downshifted and lurched the bike to a stop midway between the two men at the jeep's rear and the M-16–toting man at the front. He looked at them for a long moment, fighting back his rage as the sight of the bullet-ravaged bodies of the buck and its family filtered into his mind's eye.

Crew Cut stood. "Something we can do for you, boy?" he asked.

Heller sat in silence for another stretched second, his face a stone mask behind his sunglasses.

"No. Just passing by." Heller tried to keep his voice flat, tried to hide the anger he felt.

"Well, why don't you just keep on passin' then?" M-16 growled.

An odd grin crooked Heller's lips.

The woman tensed. She looked away from the white-haired man. White Hair kept his lust-filled gaze on the blond woman.

"I thought *Tejas* was supposed to mean friendly," Heller said. "Whatever happened to light and set?"

Crew Cut snorted. "Sounds like we got us a smartass here, Mackie."

"No, no," Heller said, smiling. "Just thought you boys might need a little help, that's all."

Crew Cut raked a curious stare over the stocks of Heller's Weatherby and 12-gauge pump shotgun.

"Tell ya how ya might help us out, cowboy," White Hair suggested, looking from Lisa to his comrades. "If yer catching my drift."

The three men chuckled.

Heller felt the woman's body dig into him from behind.

"You know how far any kind of town might be?" Heller inquired.

They just stood in hard silence.

"Nope, sure wouldn't," the big man with the M-16 drawled. "How 'bout you, boys?"

Crew Cut shook his head. His lips curled back over his teeth.

"Hell, no. See, buddy, we ain't from around these parts," White Hair said. "We came down for blacktail season. Sure you seen that, since you came this way."

"Kansas, yep, that's where we're from, boy," Crew Cut chortled.

Heller nodded shallowly.

"Well," Heller said in a cold voice as he revved the engine, "happy hunting."

He eased the chopper into the brush. Past the jeep, he dropped the bike back down onto the trail.

White Hair stepped from behind the jeep.

"Redneck assholes," Lisa muttered, her eyes glaring back at the three men.

Behind them, Crew Cut said, "I don't think we should've done let them get off that easy, Mackie."

Mackie lowered the M-16 by his side. He spat. "He wasn't nothin'. Just some bike trash. Maybe next time we see them I'll just kick the dogshit out of his smart ass."

"Nice looking tail he had with him, though," White Hair said.

"Christ, Pete, you're the horniest son of a bitch I ever met," Mackie said, an expression of disgust on his face. "You're gonna get your butt in a real sling someday because of that."

"I'll catch up to her, you watch," Pete said as the Harley vanished behind a billowing sheet of dust. "I think I'm in love!"

Mackie shook his head. "Christ. Not that shit again."

The sign read APACHE COUNTY—POPULATION 75.

Jesse Heller turned the chopper south, off Highway 54, and followed the dirt road toward the three structures that comprised the tiny town of Apache.

He steered the chopper off the road and rode a quarter of a mile out across the plain. There he parked in a gully between the hills. The dust lowered over them like a brown mist as Heller scouted the town. He found no sign of life except for the black mongrel that trotted down the center of the lone street. If the town was on the map, he decided, then it was one of the best kept secrets he'd ever seen.

Boarded-up signs on the face of a red-painted building declared it as the post office, gas station and general store. In front of the building rose an orange GULF sign that hung atop a long white pole. One gas pump stood on a concrete island.

Heller saw the telephone cable that stretched away from the trio of buildings out across the plain. It was connected to a dozen wooden poles that were spaced at quarter-mile intervals. Distance and shimmering heat swallowed up the poles.

Heller shut off the engine. "Stay here," he told her as he slid off the seat.

"And what am I supposed to do while you're socializing?"

He stared for a moment at her dust-and-dirt-smudged features. She looked old, tired.

"Keep your eyes peeled for that copter. In case we have to make a fast exit. You know how to handle one of these babies?"

A look of indignation flashed through her eyes. "In the twelve years I've been around bikers do you think all I did was pop open beer cans?"

"I don't really know what you did."

"Well, thanks for the vote of confidence."

"How'd you get so tough?" he said, a wry twist to his lips.

She shook her head as Heller walked away from her.

It was a good fifteen-minute walk across the plain to town.

The black-garbed man with the dark sunglasses stepped onto the dirt street, heading toward the general store.

The man in the rocking chair beneath the store's awning looked as old, tired and beaten as the land that surrounded Apache. When he looked up, he rolled his head in a long, lethargic motion, as if it took the old-timer a second to warm up and decide which muscle to command.

The mangy black mongrel strode out from behind an old, battered Studebaker.

With a wary gaze, Heller took in his surroundings, noting first the brown star on the window of the red brick building to his right. Printed on the door's glass in bold white letters was the word SHERIFF.

"How you doing today?" Heller called to the old-timer.

The old man studied Heller with suspicion, his eyes like

dark, watery pools behind his square-rimmed spectacles. He kept his gnarled hands clasped in his lap. The skin on his emaciated face stretched from his jowls like tanned leather pouches. A hollow space showed between his cheekbones and eye sockets.

A sad, tired face, Heller thought. *Not just old tired but a beaten soul.*

"Howdy."

Heller pulled up in front of the old man and leaned his left boot on the concrete stoop. "Sheriff around?"

"He ain't been by today."

The old man started to rock slowly back and forth in his chair. The rickety wood creaked, breaking the silence around them.

"Why you ask?"

"No reason really," Heller told him. "Just happened to run into a few boys out on the desert. Looked like they were lost. Had a little jeep trouble. Changing a flat when I saw them."

"Well, Scotty—he don't come round here much. 'Spect he might be by today, though. Mail's piling on my desk."

"Well, that's all right, I didn't need to talk to him. Say, you got a phone I can use?"

"Yar. On the counter."

"Will it call out long-distance?"

"What's long-distance?"

"L.A.," Heller said.

The old-timer perked up. An incredulous look widened his eyes. "L.A.? Shoot, you gonna have to dial in zero. That's Betty Lou over in Culberson. Runs the switchboard. Shoot, what you gonna call there for?"

Heller looked out at the gray desert. "Anybody live around here?"

"Most folks in Apache County live out in the valley. What few of us there is, that is. Sheep ranchin'." The old man peered at Heller as if noticing him for the first time. "You sure ask a lot of questions, sonny."

"Just new to the area, that's all," Heller said.

"New to the area, shoot. Ain't nobody in their right mind

moves out here. Folks that grow up here usually move to the big city. I'm last of a dying breed. Literally.''

Heller looked at the old-timer for a moment.

The old man turned his head as if Heller wasn't there anymore.

Heller stepped up onto the stoop and pushed through the door. The phone sat on the counter beside a metal cash register. Dust choked the air. Cobwebs draped from the ceiling nooks like white nets.

Heller picked up the phone, an old 1919 model with bell-shaped receiver, and blew the dust off the mouthpiece. He dialed zero.

"Operator." The woman's voice came out of the receiver.

"Yeah. I'd like to make a long-distance collect call. Area Code two one three, five seven four, five one eighty-eight.''

"And your name, please.''

"Jesse.''

"The number you're calling from, sir?''

"Uh.'' Heller looked at the phone but found no number. "I'm calling from the general store in Apache.''

He heard the phone ring three times before the click on the other end told him someone had picked it up.

"Hello?''

Heller felt the tension stir inside of him as he heard the tired, familiar voice of his bail bondsman and wartime friend, Vinnie Tyson.

"I have a collect call from Jesse. Will you accept the charge?''

There was a tight pause on the other end. Heller could almost see the anger stretching out the skin on his friend's gaunt face.

"Sir? Will you accept the call?''

"Come on, Vinnie. Cut the crap.''

"Yes, I'll pay for the call, operator.''

Heller heard the operator disconnect her line.

A long moment of cold silence passed.

"Well, Jesse, how many guys have you killed today?''

Heller's spine stiffened as he detected the ice in Tyson's voice. "I guess you've heard.''

"Heard?"

Tyson's voice boomed out of the receiver as if he were just in the other room instead of fifteen hundred miles away.

"Jesus, Jesse. Is that the dumbest thing you can think of to say? Your name's splattered all over the news. The FBI has already been here. Twice! Interrogated me—for days, it seemed. And you ask me if I've heard. That takes balls."

"They got the phone tapped?"

"No. That's what I listened for when I first picked it up. But do you really care?"

Heller leaned his elbows on the counter. He clamped his eyelids shut and massaged the bridge of his nose with his right thumb and forefinger. "Listen, Vinnie—"

"No, you listen, Jesse. I warned you before you did it not to go after those bikers. Now it's too late. Not only have you thrown your own life away, but the feds might haul me off for aiding and abetting a known felon."

"Come on, Vinnie. That's only talk. You've been around long enough to know they're just applying a little pressure."

"A little pressure, huh? Well, the feds dropped off a court-ordered injunction on my desk two hours ago. Are those just words too? I don't cooperate, they yank my ticket. Means I'm out of business."

"I might need some running money, Vinnie."

"What?"

"You got any jumpers up north, say Illinois, Indiana? You've got other skip tracers working for you. I could catch the jumper, turn him over. . . . ."

"You are crazy, you know that? I got a business here to run, damn you. A business your little vengeance excursion has seriously jeopardized. How do you think I'll hold my life together if they take that away? A disabled vet doesn't get a whole bunch of chances in the World, Jesse."

Heller felt sorry for his friend. He knew Tyson was right—his friend might not get another chance to make it in society.

The Vietnam War had brought them together. A Cong ambush had wiped out most of the men in Heller's squad. A mine blast had nearly killed Tyson, sheared his right arm off at the shoulder. Heller could still hear his friend's screams, the cries of the other dying soldiers, tortured voices that burned through his mind like nails scratching over chalkboard.

Heller and a man named Ben Williams had driven back the Cong surge until a medevac chopper had arrived.

Heller wondered whatever became of Ben Williams.

"Is this call meant to be some sort of an apology?"

Heller's mind drifted back to the present. Tyson's sharp voice seemed to drill out of the receiver. Heller winced.

"I don't have any choice, Vinnie. I've got nothing left but to keep on running. I did what I felt was right, what I believed. Right now I've got a girl with me who saw some bikers murder a Congressman's kid over drugs. They've already sent some outlaws after us; they'll send others. So it looks like they might just keep on coming after me until they finally get me—and the girl."

"So why call me? Just to say, Hi, how you doin'?"

A sad smile touched Heller's lips. It suddenly dawned on him that there really was no escape, that the path he had chosen—or had the path chosen him? he wondered—would more than likely lead him to his death, a violent, horrible death. He wondered if this was how a man walking to the gallows felt in his last few minutes.

"I just called to see if you were all right."

The .357 magnum swung up behind Heller's head.

"I hope—"

"Freeze, boy."

Heller's mouth hung open. He felt the gun barrel's cold steel as if it were the sharp tip of an icicle jabbing into the nape of his neck. Heller didn't recognize the voice, but he sensed the threatening presence of a man quite prepared to blow his head off.

"Don't you make any funny moves, boy."

"Jesse? Jesse?"

Tyson's voice shot out of the receiver, loud and hollow in the taut silence.

Heller felt his heart hammer against his chest. He heard the revolver's hammer click back.

8

"JUST EASE THAT phone down. Real slow."

"Jesse? What in . . ."

Heller hung up the receiver and turned around slowly. He stood toe to toe, eye level with Sheriff McClan. They stared at each other through dark sunglasses.

Heller found himself facing a square-shouldered, heavily muscled man. He cursed himself for having let his mind wander. He should have been alert to the sounds of voices and car doors slamming. But hindsight was for men who could afford it, not for a man living on the edge of death.

"Is that him, Scotty? Is that him?"

Heller shifted his gaze to the tall, blubbery deputy behind McClan. Sweat soaked the fat deputy's brown shirt in large wet splotches. A Smith & Wesson Model 29.44 magnum quivered in his fleshy right hand.

"Yeah, Junior," the sheriff of Apache County gloated. "I reckon we got us Jesse Heller."

"What do we do now, Scotty?" asked a second deputy, who was short and redheaded. This deputy brandished a long-barreled .38 revolver.

"We're gonna hand Jesse here over to the feds, Dumpy. Yup. Imagine that. We just nabbed us the biggest outlaw the state of Texas has ever seen.'' McClan stepped aside. ''They say you's a man to ride the rivers with, Jesse.''

''He don't look so tough now, does he, Scotty?''

''Shut up, Junior,'' McClan chided. ''Gun was in the other hand, you'd be blubbering like a baby with a diaper full of doo-doo. Damned good thing we don't never go blowing into someplace like the seventh cavalry or he might have that gun now.''

Heller stood there and looked at the four men in cold silence.

''Gimme your cuffs, Junior.''

Junior's jaw slackened. ''Cuffs?''

''Yeah, your cuffs, dammit!''

Junior's jaw slackened. ''Cuffs?''

''Yeah, your cuffs, dammit!''

''I left them in the car.''

McClan scowled. ''Dumpy?''

''Geez, Scotty, I guess I left mine too.''

''Good place for them. Next time why don't you stay there with them. What would you do if you're— Ah, never mind. Frig it.'' McClan waved his revolver. ''Let's us step outside, Jess. Easy now. I don't want to plug you. Can't mess you up for the picture the boys'll take of us.''

The old man backed away from the door, stood on the stoop as Heller stepped past the three lawmen.

The magnum in Junior's hand shook as if he were holding a jackhammer.

''Dammit, Junior, put that thing away 'fore you kill somebody,'' McClan rasped.

Heller walked through the doorway.

McClan led his deputies outside. ''Toward the vehiculars, Jess.''

Junior and Dumpy wore expressions of triumph. They slid revolvers into their holsters.

Heller looked at the two brown squad cars parked across the street in front of the sheriff's office.

''All right, hold it!''

The voice sounded like a rifle shot crackling down the street.

Heller stopped. The three lawmen froze in their tracks, looking as if they'd just walked into a quicksand bog.

Lisa Stephens pumped the slide action on the Smith & Wesson 12-gauge. She kept the barrel trained on McClan's back. "Drop the gun, Sheriff."

Heller turned and plucked the .357 out of McClan's hand.

"Sheriff," Junior said.

"Raise those hands, fatty," she barked. "You too, stubby."

Junior and Dumpy lifted their arms. They seemed uncertain, as if the woman would blast them no matter what they did.

Heller snapped open the magnum's cylinder and shook the cartridges from the chamber. He flung the emptied revolver down the street.

The woman sidestepped away from the group, toward the squad cars as Heller unholstered Junior's magnum and Dumpy's .38. He opened the cylinders on both revolvers and let the shells tumble to the dirt. He looked at Lisa with a strange, fleeting smile of gratitude.

She seemed pleased with herself.

McClan turned to face the shotgun-toting woman. He drew in a deep breath. Placing his hands on his hips, he looked at Heller. He seemed momentarily amused about something. "Killing outlaw bikers is one thing, boy. Killing lawmen in the state of Texas is something else. Something real, real bad. Called murder."

Heller pitched both revolvers behind him. "I'm not going to kill anybody."

"Sheriff," Dumpy said in a tentative voice. "We ain't gonna let them get away with this, are we?"

McClan ignored his deputy. "I may look like some hicktown, shit-for-brains redneck lawman to you, buddy, but I swear to Jesus I'm gonna nail you myself."

Heller stood in silence.

The old man seemed to look at Heller with indifference, but he allowed a chuckle and shook his head. "New to the area, eh?"

"What the hell's so funny, Compton?" McClan growled, his voice sour.

"Shoot, Scotty. If this is the fella that burned them bikers, I say pin a gold star on his chest and let him ride."

Heller took the shotgun out of the woman's grasp. Gently, he wrapped his right hand around her arm and led her down the street away from the group.

"That fella done what I shoulda years ago. 'Member when that pack of animals came through here? Leveled my place. Damn near destroyed the valley. Shoot-poot, let the fella scoot."

McClan showed the old man a ferocious look.

"Sheriff?"

McClan swung his sharp expression toward Junior.

Junior pointed. "They're getting away."

McClan wheeled and scooped up the loose shells.

Heller and the woman jogged side by side out onto the plain.

Heller heard car doors slam shut. He turned and stopped.

The woman grinned. "Don't worry. I took care of that," she told him as McClan slid into his cruiser. "A few ripped wires. A lot of dirt in the carburetor. No radio. Should hold them for a while, I think."

"You're crazy, you know that?" he said, listening as the engines of both cruisers choked out. "Now you're in as deep as I am."

"Maybe I decided I like you," she said. "Can I do that— like you?"

Heller looked at her. "Where's the bike?"

"I left it."

McClan burst out of his car, banged the door shut. "You're finished, boy!" he fumed. He waggled his hand. Spittle sprayed out of his mouth.

Junior and Dumpy stepped out of the cruisers and stood unmoving, afraid of the sheriff's livid rage.

"You hear me? I'll get you for this. I'll step on you like the snake you are."

The old man chuckled. "C'mon, Scotty. Lighten up some.

You gonna get your blood pressure all up, blow your brains out yer ears all over the street.''

McClan spun toward the old man and shouted, "Shut up. SHUT UP!''

The old man hooked his thumbs behind his belt buckle.

"Shoot, Scotty. What you gettin' so worked up for?''

McClan snatched his Stetson off his head and hurled it against the back windshield of the cruiser. He kicked at the ground.

Heller lowered the shotgun by his leg. "Come on, let's go,'' he said.

They began running across the plain.

"I'm comin' after you, boy! I'll dig through every cave. I'll turn up every rock. You won't get away! You hear me? GOD DAMN YOU!''

The old man's soft chuckling rolled out across the desert after the retreating man and woman.

But Jesse Heller wasn't laughing.

A fierce wind struck the single-rotor helicopter, shimmying the whirlybird as if it were nothing more than a child's toy.

"We can't go down there!'' the pilot shouted to the police marksman next to him.

Like giant knives, the towering peaks of the Guadalupe Mountains parted the billowing stratus clouds as they boiled down into the gorge. The canyon looked like an endless sea of cottonballs.

The marksman seemed disappointed. A pair of binoculars dangled from the strap around his neck. A Steyr-Mannlicher .30-06 high-powered rifle with an infrared telescopic sight sat across his lap.

The pilot pulled the cyclic pitch stick to him and swung the chopper left.

"We'll never find him down there, Mike!'' The rotor's noise and the wind blowing through the cockpit seemed to sweep the pilot's words out of the open door of the bubble-shaped Plexiglas. "If he's in there, the park police will let us know. I'm not going to chance smashing us off those cliffs in this weather. It's not worth it.''

Mike mouthed a curse. One hand tightened around the Mannlicher. He reached for the radio mike. "Buck Morris ain't gonna like it."

"Hell with that," the pilot growled. "I'm setting her down someplace. I'm hungry anyway."

A frown pinched in the marksman's cheeks.

The two-way radio crackled beside Buck Morris.

"Eagle One to Ground Run. Acknowledge. Over."

Morris kept his left hand on the steering wheel, his eyes on the road as he reached for the mike. "This is Ground One. What do you know, Mike?"

"No sign of the subject, Buck. We got as far as Pine Springs, but Dewey can't fly in 'cause of the clouds. And he keeps crying about his empty belly."

Morris showed gritted teeth. "It's getting on in the day, Mike. It'll be dark soon. You've been out there for eight hours and you still haven't seen a thing."

"Sorry, Buck. Hell, it ain't hard for a man to lose himself in those mountains. There must be a hundred places a man can hide down there—*if* he's down there. I think you're gonna have to call in the Rangers on this one, Buck. I know you'd rather not do that, but that range'll have to be gone through on horse and jeep."

"Well, keep searching."

"Any luck there?"

Morris' knuckles gleamed white as he tightened his hold on the steering wheel. The mike shook a little in his hand, as if he wanted to crush the instrument into powdered dust. "I got a situation, maybe. Leroy radioed about an hour ago. A pack of bikers headed west on the interstate. I got a roadblock up just outside Van Horn to intercept them."

"Trouble?"

"I think so."

"How many?"

"Thirty. They're armed too."

Morris heard the soft whistle come through the transmitter. He felt a sudden stab of annoyance with his helicopter team and wondered if they were just up there telling dirty jokes, killing time. "Keep me posted by the hour. And stay up there, all right?"

"Gotcha, Buck."

"Out."

Morris hung the mike back up beside the transmitter. He mashed down on the gas pedal, weaved over into the left lane, shot past the slower traffic in front of him.

Something seemed to tug at his stomach. He knew something was wrong. Trouble, he knew, waited for no man. Violence, he had seen, often erupted without warning, like a sudden cloudburst.

Like the time in Vietnam when he had seen three ten-year-old girls offer the men of the Seventh SFG bowls of rice. Except hand grenades had been planted beneath the rice and had blown the heads off five men.

Buck Morris sucked in a deep breath and pushed the horrible memory from his mind. Pete chugged down the beer and flung the empty bottle out the passenger window of the jeep. He belched as the jeep's wheels bounced over rock. The sudden jolt lifted him six inches off the seat. He came down and toppled over the metal cooler.

"Easy there, Butch. I still got some fuckin' to get in under the belt yet."

The crew-cut driver laughed. "Been awhile since you notched yourself one, ain't it, Petie Sketie. Hell, Mackie, I bet Pete's got the cleanest cock in Texas. I bet you could perform open-heart surgery with that thing."

Mackie and Butch laughed hard.

Pete ignored his comrades. "Hey, look there. What's that?" he said.

The three men looked out across the desert.

A line of dust followed the small, dark shape of the black Harley-Davidson chopper. The bike went west, opposite their direction.

"Looks like our smartass bikin' buddy," Butch said. "What do you think, Mackie? When's the last time you worked out on somebody's skull?"

Mackie took a swig out of a bottle of Old Grand Dad bourbon and studied the bike as it streaked past their field of vision a quarter mile in the distance.

"You know that crack he made about happy hunting?" Pete said, eyelids narrowing over a steely, glinting stare. "He might just decide to tell the sheriff about them dead deer. Mc-Clan got real riled the last time."

"That's only 'cause you went shootin' old man Twamley's sheep, knucklehead," Mackie rasped. His voice was slurred by alcohol, his eyes glassy and mean looking.

"He didn't know it was us," Pete defended himself.

"Damned good thing he didn't," Mackie shot back. "They'd a run us out of the county with butts full of buckshot."

"Well, what do you think, Mackie?" Butch pressed, voice taut.

The jeep jarred through a rut, throwing them off balance. Mackie banged the back of his head on the door.

"I think I'm feeling kind of mean and nasty, boys." Mackie took another swallow of bourbon. His eyes burned. "I think maybe our bikin' buddy needs to get taught a little lesson in Texas manners. I feel like kickin' some butt too."

The white-haired Pete let out a low, harsh chuckle. He picked up a .22 Marlin rifle.

Butch laughed. Grinding the gears as he downshifted, he swung the steering wheel.

Heller looked into his side-view mirror and saw the black Renegade jeep lunge up over a rise to bounce down on the desert floor.

The jeep began to cut like a scythe through the Harley's trail of thick dust.

The white-haired man leaned out of the window and Heller saw the rifle's muzzle flash a millisecond before he heard the crack of the gunshot.

Lisa flinched as the bullet whined off the stone next to her.

Heller sent the bike up the smooth face of an embedded boulder and shot off the lip of the rock like a rocket. The airborne bike slammed down on its tires, nearly throwing Heller and the woman from the seat as he fought to keep the bars from wrenching out of his hands.

The jeep suddenly accelerated.

Heller saw the laughing faces loom up in his side mirror like weird Halloween masks.

"Hey, boy! How's the happy hunting now?" Mackie hollered.

The terrain rolled in front of Heller. Dangerous, deep ruts seemed to appear out of nowhere.

The jeep lurched forward, coming within inches of the chopper's back tire and forcing Heller to gun the throttle. The Harley shot away from the Renegade's front fender, spewing out a gray ball of dust.

"Yahoooooooo!"

Mackie fired another three-round burst, aiming over the couple's heads.

Heller ducked instinctively. Adrenaline burned like acid through his veins. As he glanced in the mirror, he felt the front end of the bike jump up as the ground rose.

"Look out!" the woman shouted in his ear.

Heller saw the spiny arms of a cactus rush at him. He threw his weight left, twisted the bars. A prickly needle ripped down along his arm, opening a long streak of torn flesh. Lisa screamed an instant before the chopper's front end pounded into a large rock. The bike's back end flipped up and the sky, the desert, the hills spun in a gray haze in Heller's vision as he went over the high side.

The woman fell off to the side, plunging into the hard-packed soil and rolling several yards down the hill.

The Harley slammed down into the hillside, the impact hurtling the saddlebag far from the bike as Heller sailed down the hill, hammering into the ground.

He tumbled, his flailing arms and legs punching out clouds of dust. The back of his head smacked stone and a white flash of lightning blazed in his mind.

The jeep skidded to a jerky halt along the rise.

Mackie opened the door. He looked fearful for a moment as he stepped out onto the hill, gripping his M-16.

Butch and Pete jumped out the door. Dust from behind the jeep rolled over the three men.

Several seconds of hard silence passed.

The woman, stretched on her stomach, lifted her face out of the dirt and drew herself up on her hands and knees.

The white-haired Pete nodded toward Heller. "Go check him," he said, his voice cracking with tension.

Quickly, Mackie stepped down the hill, keeping the M-16 pointed at Heller's motionless form.

Heller heard the footsteps. The crunching sound seemed to echo in his ears, coming from miles off. A warm stickiness trickled down his neck. He groaned and moved his left arm.

Mackie launched the toe of his boot into Heller's gut. The blow flipped Heller on his back.

Lisa clambered to her feet. Her knees shook. Dust streaked her face. "What do you assholes want?"

Heller looked up at the big man's leering face hovering over him through a blurry fog.

"Hell, he's all right," Mackie said, sounding cheerful as he drove the heel of his boot down onto Heller's cheek, knocking him back against the ground. "Now."

Heller heard their voices, a crackling, distorted maze of noise in his head.

"Look at this, will ya?"

Butch showed them the Uzi, his expression like that of a child on Christmas morning.

"What else has he got in there?" Mackie asked. "He got any money?"

Butch slid the Weatherby from its sheath, examined it and tossed it up to Pete.

"Sheeit," Butch gasped, pulling the stainless-steel Ruger New Super Blackhawk .44 magnum from Heller's saddlebag, then holding up the sticks of dynamite. "For bike trash this boy's packing enough hardware to wipe out the next ten counties."

Pete looked at the woman and grinned. He took a step toward her. As she took a step back, she stumbled over a rock. Pete snatched her toward him. "C'mere, sugah."

She swung and cracked an open palm off the man's face.

Pete's white mane swept out and around like a half-opened umbrella as he twisted his head away.

"Stupid bitch!" he snarled and felled her with a backhand to her jaw.

"Christ, Petie," Mackie griped. "You gonna fuck her or beat her to death?"

Pete wrenched her arm. She yelped as he hauled her off the ground. He tossed her toward the jeep, the momentum sending her staggering off balance. Blood trickled down from the left corner of her mouth.

Mackie held the pump shotgun in his free hand, studied it and looked back down at Heller.

Butch rattled the heavy chain, tossing it aside. "Jee-zus Christ." He pulled two fat wads of green cash out of the saddlebag. His gaze widened.

Mackie reached out and grabbed the money. He tucked the M-16 and shotgun under his left arm and with quick fingers leafed through the crisp ends of the bills. "These are all hundreds, thousand-dollar bills. Any more in there?"

Butch rifled through the saddlebag. He pulled out a round gold-edged case that fit snugly in his palm like a pocket watch. He opened the case and saw a woman's portrait staring up at him. Her blue eyes seemed to flash with warmth, her smile wide, friendly.

Butch flung the pocket portrait away from him, snarling. The glass cracked as the frame hit stone.

"Naw. There ain't no more," he said as he dropped the saddlebag by his feet. "Who the hell you think he is anyway?"

Mackie looked at Heller.

Butch seemed confused. He shifted his gaze from Heller to Mackie to the white-haired Pete.

"I don't know," Mackie said. "Bikers, they ain't."

Anger flared in Pete's eyes. His left cheek was still red from the woman's blow. "Then what are they?"

"How should I know?" Mackie snapped. He trudged up the hill.

Pete had his hand wrapped around the woman's arm. He shook her.

She lashed out, but Pete grabbed her other wrist. He showed his comrades a lopsided grin. "We got us a real wildfire hellcat here, boys. Tell you what," he suggested. "We got some brews left. Why don't we take her on up in the hills out of sight? He nodded toward Heller. "He'll still be here when we get back. We'll ask him about it all then, when he wakes up."

Mackie seemed set to protest the idea. He appeared to ponder for a moment, gazing at his white-haired companion. He looked at the woman and a smile broke his lips. He laughed and the other two men joined his laughter.

Lisa looked down at Jesse Heller. "Jesse?" Pain stretched the skin taut across her face. She cried as she was jerked toward the jeep.

"Jump in, sugah," Pete growled, shoving her into the jeep.

The sound of the jeep's engine firing to life penetrated the throbbing in Heller's head. He forced open his eyelids and saw the jeep back away from the edge of the hill and disappear.

9

JESSE HELLER WAS no stranger to pain and suffering.

He had known pain throughout much of his adult life—intense, burning, unrelenting pain. It was something dark and twisted inside of him that lay in his guts, hot like butter melting over a stove's flame. Physical pain, like what he was now experiencing as he lifted himself into a sitting position, he could take without much thought or care; it was something every man who carried his own weight in the world dealt with. But emotional anguish was something entirely different. That, he knew, was something that didn't heal like the closing of a knife wound. The unseen scars never seemed to heal, but rather faded deep inside a man with the passage of time.

And the torture lived on inside Jesse Heller, buried just beneath the surface.

He felt it every time he saw the faces of his murdered family as they haunted his memory. Every time he remembered the horrible, violent deaths of comrades in Vietnam.

He looked up the hill and saw his downed bike and discarded saddlebag. He felt the fear crawl through him.

They had stolen his weapons. They had taken the woman. And he was certain they had found the ten thousand dollars he had seized from the Satan's Avengers, part of the money he had used to plot, then enact his revenge against the killers of his family.

He winced as he felt the opened skin on the back of his skull pulse beneath a matted patch of hair. Dust caked his clothes, face, neck.

He now recalled their words, the voices that had seemed to call from inside his head as he had lain on the threshold of unconsciousness.

Hills. Brews. Still be here when we get back.

Heller stood with effort. The pain seemed to swell through his muscles. He looked at the long cut that ran down his right arm. Dirt and sweat mingled with his blood, and the wound stung as if countless bees had attacked his flesh.

As Heller took a step up the hill, his boot crunched something. He stopped and looking down, felt his gut wrenched by anger and grief. He knelt and picked up the pocket portrait in his hand. The dark purple bruise under his left eye seemed to fade as the color drained out of his features.

A lump caught in his throat. His gaze misted over with a look of sorrow.

He stared for long moments at the woman's face, the woman he would have married, the woman who had been raped and butchered two weeks before he came back from Vietnam. His lips parted.

"Julie."

He wasn't sure if he had spoken her name, for a voice always seemed to be saying her name over and over in his mind.

Her image was distorted grotesquely by the cracked glass. Gently, he tapped out the splintered fragments and rubbed the dust off the gold edges of the casing. She had been the most beautiful woman he had ever seen; the kindest, gentlest, most understanding person he'd ever known. He wanted to remember her that way. He felt life had shamed her because of the horrible way she had died—but he knew she had nothing to be ashamed of. His memory of her was pure and warm, his dreams of her at night filled with longing.

He gazed at her deep blue eyes, heard her voice. He could almost feel the tender touch of her hands on his face.

"Jesse, I'm scared. I don't want you to leave."

Her voice seemed to echo in on him from the surrounding desert.

"I love you, Jesse boy. I'll wait for you."

The hurt welled up in his chest. Her face became a blur as he looked out from behind the veil of moisture that filmed his eyes.

"I'll be here for you when you come home, Jesse. I love you so much."

His stare dropped as he hung his head and shut his eyes. He rubbed his eyes with his thumb and forefinger. He felt his shoulders tremble. Only he would ever know that he grieved like this. His pain was a lonely thing, not to be shared.

Heller rose slowly and sucked in a deep breath. He put her portrait in his pants pocket. He felt as if a great weight had dropped on his shoulders, and he stood there for a stretched second, as if rooted to the ground. He shifted his gaze, saw his broken sunglasses crushed to slivers in the dust.

He walked to the saddlebag. It was empty. They had taken everything. Guns. Money. Dynamite.

He feared what they would do to the woman.

He knew he wouldn't just ride away and leave her to fend for herself. There was something about her he liked, some intangible quality in her character he couldn't quite understand but admired. Perhaps it was her gutsiness, her ability to keep picking herself up when fate seemed determined to knock her flat on her ass.

He didn't know how far ahead they'd gotten, but he would follow the ruts the jeep tires had left. He would track them down.

He had seen their kind before. Vicious men driven by impulses and dark feelings they made no attempt to understand, control or hide. Local rednecks with nothing but time on their hands, trouble on their minds. It hadn't been the first time a man had wished to kick the hell out of him for just breathing the same air. He knew it was senseless, that perhaps there really was such a thing as evil. He had been confronted before by men who had wanted to beat or to kill him simply because he rode a motorcycle. Perhaps they had seen him as some criminal on the run. Perhaps they had envied the freedom he seemed to enjoy.

Heller draped the empty saddlebag over the sissy bar. He saw that the headlamp was shattered, the left handlebar dented and bent slightly. He inspected the engine but saw no oil leakage and found nothing on the engine cracked.

He looked at the chain that lay in the dust several yards away from the chopper. He picked it up. The metal felt cold on his skin as he wrapped the heavy chain around his forearm, wrist, hand. A grim look darkened his expression. His jaw clenched. If they hurt the woman, they would pay. He wouldn't allow her to suffer like Julie had.

Heller turned, walked back to the chopper. He set the chopper upright and climbed onto the saddle. The other side-view mirror had been smashed off by the fall.

He jumped down on the kick starter. Nothing. He tried three times before the bike sputtered to life and spat out black exhaust. He twisted the throttle, gunning the engine.

He slipped the bike into gear and eased out on the clutch. The front tire scrunched over the sunglasses as Heller wheeled the big bike around. He rode up the rise and vanished down the other side of the hill.

They rode straight out of the dark horizon, demons from hell descending on the highway, the noise of choppers a tortured roar from the maw of eternal damnation.

The Sinners' formation took up both lanes of the interstate. Buzz Swann rode his Panhead over the white lane divider, ahead of and between the two lines of outlaw bikers. He was relaxed as he led the pack, thundering down the highway at a steady fifty-five miles per hour.

Most of the Sinners rode early-model bikes they'd restored, as if holding on to the memory of the past. Knuckleheads and Flatheads with foot clutch and tank shift; Sportsters with six-over front ends, upsweep pipes, lowered and stretched; handlebars that ranged from early Electra Glide to stock western and Triumph ram's horns; front wheels reaching out on long forks; primary outer covers and pipes made

of gold; chrome so finely polished it could mirror a man as
he shaved himself.

The bald-headed Mad Mike straddled a '66 Shovelhead
with a flaming red paint job. Chains crossed the chest of his
denim jacket like a bandit's bandoliers.

Turd beamed astride a '74 model Sportster. He'd designed
and built his scooter's hydraulic clutch to stretch more mile-
age out of the eighty-six-cubic-inch engine so that he
wouldn't have to constantly look down at the generator light
on every long run.

The amassed engine roar sounded like peals of rolling
thunder, warning cars ahead of the pack of oncoming Sinners.

A station wagon with Florida plates and luggage roped
across the roof pulled off onto the shoulder of the highway.

A skinny man with a pink visor, thick eyeglasses and a Ha-
waiian shirt hopped out of the driver's side. He lifted a Nikon
camera to his face as the formation closed down on him. The
wagon's back window rolled down, and two boys watched
the bikers. They threw their hands up over their ears, looked
at each other and laughed.

"Henry! Get back in this car!" the man's wife screeched,
but the din of engine noise washed over her voice. "Those
hoodlums . . ."

Henry clicked the camera.

Swann roared past the station wagon and glanced at the vacationer with an expression of smug indifference.

Mad Mike hollered. His eyes appeared on the verge of
popping out of his head. He waved a middle finger at the
camera as he roared past on his Shovelhead. "Your wife pulls
trains!"

"Henry!"

Turd made a face for the camera.

Henry snapped a picture of Turd.

Chaos spat on the station wagon.

Lobo veered his Flathead off the road. The vacationer
flung himself back against the car, aghast, as the chopper
swept past him, missing the opened driver's door by inches.
The door quivered on its hinges in the slipstream.

Bobo smashed a beer bottle off the asphalt. Glass chips pelted the wagon's side.

A quarter of a mile down the road, Swann led his men past a rest stop.

A carload of girls shouted and waved at the bikers. There was a University of Texas banner across the back of their new Volvo.

Swann grinned but the expression disappeared as he looked into his side-view mirror and saw a dozen Sinners fall out of formation and swing into the rest stop's lot.

"What the shit!" he rasped. "This ain't no goddamned fuckin' joyride!"

He motioned with his arm for the formation to pull off onto the shoulder. As scooters slowed and rolled off the road, the Sinner leader wheeled around and hit the throttle. The Panhead looked like a missile, a blue streak of lightning shooting back down the center of the highway.

A four-door Buick Regal blared its horn at Swann as the chopper bore down on the car.

Swann shifted his weight left and swung wide.

Tire rubber squealed. The Buick skidded off the highway, trailing a long line of white smoke.

Swann rode into the rest stop.

"C'mon, let's head out, baby," Saldado Mars, a lean, handsome biker suggested in a loud voice to a blond girl in a green Izod shirt.

The twelve Sinners formed a circle around the Volvo with their scooters.

The four girls shared nervous grins while the guy that was with them sat in the driver's seat looking as if he'd just stepped into a pit of vipers.

The group of bikers looked up as Swann braked the Panhead to a long, slow halt. They looked at Swann like children prepared to receive a stern reprimand from their father.

"What the shit's wrong with you guys?" Swann wore an expression halfway between disgust and amusement. He jerked a thumb over his shoulder. "This ain't no orgy. Get the lead out!"

The four girls seemed instantly relieved. The guy looked

as if he'd just released his bladder. One of the girls sounded a nervous giggle.

Swann clenched his jaw, put his left hand on his hip and watched as the outlaws rolled past him.

"Sorry, Buzz. Thought we had us some sheep here," Saldado Mars said. "Got a little excited, that's all."

"Yeah, yeah, sure. Don't pull this kinda shit again!" he shouted after his men, face flushed with anger. He looked at the girls and grinned. *Yeah, definitely sheep,* he thought.

"Have to excuse the boys. They fall in love easy," Swann said. He popped out the clutch, hit the throttle and squeezed the hand brake. The Panhead's back end spun around in a half-doughnut.

The blonde covered her ears and grimaced as Swann raced out of the lot.

The jeep topped the rocky hill and shuddered to a stop along the crest.

Butch flung open his door. He tossed an empty beer bottle down the hill. Glass shattered. He belched.

Pete was working on his twelfth beer. He shoved Lisa between the two front seats and she banged her knee against the metal stick shift.

Mackie greeted the woman's cry with harsh laughter.

The big man snatched her by the sleeve of her jacket and dragged her out through the door. She tried to wrestle free of his hold, but this seemed to only enrage Mackie. He slung her down, sending her slamming off a rock and rolling across the ground.

Pete squeezed out the door. He looked down at the fallen woman. "Easy, Mackie. I know she ain't no vestal virgin, but I don't want her bleeding all over me. Damn, dude."

She looked up. Hair fell across her face. She held her left elbow, massaging the arm. Defiance blazed in her eyes.

Mackie glowered. He hurled his beer bottle at a wall of rock. Butch stepped from around in front of the jeep, buckling on the black leather gunbelt he'd stolen from Jesse Heller. He grinned as he pulled the Ruger .44 magnum from its hip holster. The crew-cut man held the stainless-steel cannon carefully, gazing at it in awe.

"You happy now that you got a new toy?" Mackie growled.

Butch looked away from Mackie and nodded at the woman. "I sure hope a little piece makes you not so hostile."

Pete chugged beer.

Mackie turned an angry expression on the woman. "Your boyfriend wasn't as tough as he thought he was, bitch, was he?" he rasped. "Just a smart mouthpiece of bikin' trash was all he was." He drew a large buck knife from a sheath beneath his sheepskin coat.

Butch's eyes went wide with horror.

Pete froze.

The woman's mouth went slack.

In a lightning-swift move, Mackie grabbed the woman's right sleeve and slashed the knife across it. "Hell's this?" he spat, his face twisted in a vindictive snarl as the blade tore through leather. Mackie gouged out the American flag with a wrenching slice of the blade. "Goddamned commie disgrace." He threw the severed patch into her face.

Lisa bolted up off the ground, running for the rocks.

Pete sucked the beer bottle dry. He cursed and tossed the bottle after the woman.

She flinched as glass exploded off the rock next to her face. She stumbled and pitched to the ground.

Pete moved for the woman with long strides.

She twisted around, a fear-crazed stare in her eyes.

Mackie took several steps away from Butch. "Why don't you grab us a couple of brews, Butchie. Might as well have us a party while we're waiting for studly there."

Pete pounced on the woman, draping his body over her in a heavy blanket of arms and legs that pinned her to the ground. She squirmed beneath him, a look of revulsion contorting her features.

"Come on, sugah." Pete's tone was pleading. "It's not so bad, is it?"

"With a real man it wouldn't be," she rasped.

Pete showed her a wolfish grin, but she wiped the expression off his face with an open palm slap.

Mackie winced, then smiled at the sound of the cracking blow. "Having some trouble there, Mister Ladykiller," he mocked.

Long, thick strands of white hair tumbled across Pete's face. His expression of rage was demonic. He shook her violently and backhanded her in the face.

Mackie glanced over his shoulder.

Butch, walking down the outside of the jeep, skirted the hill's edge. He faced the front of the jeep and tugged down his zipper.

"Hurry it up with those beers, will ya?"

"You're that damned thirsty, get them yourself. Can't I even piss in peace without a bunch of bitching?"

Mackie glanced over his shoulder at Butch. He shook his head in disgust and turned away from his crew-cut comrade. As Mackie watched Pete wrestle with Lisa, he grew impatient.

The man named Pete slapped the woman hard, twice. She lay still, defeated, her eyes glazed.

Butch pulled up his zipper. A pleased expression on his face, he looked at Mackie's broad backside.

"You done yet, or maybe you're gonna take a dump now?" Mackie growled out of the corner of his mouth.

"Yeah, yeah, yeah," Butch griped. He turned around and froze.

A depthless fury burned in Jesse Heller's eyes.

Butch stood unmoving, clearly unnerved by the expression beneath the bruised and bloodied face in front of him. The self-satisfied smirk the crew-cut man wore instantly melted into a look of shock, as if he'd just seen his life pass before his eyes.

Heller felt his rage fueled by the woman's soft cries. Tortured memories reached out from the dark recesses of his mind. He searched the crew-cut man's eyes for a split second and saw in the other's expression the look of a man who knew he'd committed a grave injustice, the look of a man who knew he deserved to die.

Butch reached a trembling hand for the Ruger magnum.

Heller lifted his chain-wrapped left fist. His face twisted into a snarl, his lips drew back over gritted teeth. He seemed to drag the moment out on purpose, as if daring Butch to pull the Ruger and gun him down.

Then Heller drilled his fist square into the man's mouth, throwing every bit of his strength into the blow. He felt the man's teeth snap off under the terrible impact, as if he'd hammered into icicles instead of flesh and bone. Butch's jawbone shattered. Blood and bone sprayed from his ruined face.

The crew-cut man crumpled.

"Hey, Butch, what the hell's taking so long? Damn, boy, I swear."

Heller ducked down behind the jeep. Stretching out flat on his stomach, he rolled beneath the jeep without a sound. He saw Mackie turn and walk to the back of the vehicle. Out of his peripheral vision, Heller caught the white-haired man's movements as he tugged the leather jacket off Lisa.

Heller crawled to the back of the jeep on his hands and knees. His head missed the tailpipe by an inch as he squeezed between the back tires.

Mackie stopped by the left rear side.

The big man stared at his outstretched comrade, the blood that slicked his face like a wet mask.

Heller lunged up, struck like a snake from brush.

Mackie's eyes widened. His mouth opened.

Heller dropped the chain over the man's head, wrapped it around his neck and squeezed. He used the fear, the anger he felt, and pulled the chain tighter, strangling Mackie's cry of alarm.

The big man gagged. Spittle ran down his lips. His tongue became a black-and-purple lump that lolled out of his mouth.

The veins in Heller's arms pumped up with blood and adrenaline. His biceps bulged, rippling like thick corded knots as he applied lethal pressure.

Mackie's knees buckled, but he reached up for Heller and grabbed a handful of hair.

Pete finally slapped the fight out of Lisa with another open-palm slap. She stared up at her tormentor, her eyes brimming with tears. An ugly red welt shone on the right side of her mouth. A rivulet of blood snaked down her chin.

Heller felt the sudden surge of power in Mackie's upper body as the big man fought in desperation to hold on to his life. Mackie cupped his right hand around the back of Heller's skull.

Heller gnashed his teeth, veins popping out on his forehead like blue worms. He dug inside himself for strength and forced the bigger man to his knees with a downward wrenching motion of his arms.

Pete pulled the zipper down on the woman's pants.

She seemed delirious, submitting as the man grabbed a handful of her jeans and panties and yanked.

Mackie's eyes strained from their sockets. His face reddened, turning a dark shade of crimson.

Heller drove the big man's face into the side of the jeep. He pulled back on the chain, thrust down and banged Mackie's head off the fender. Heller slid the chain from around the big man's neck. Mackie's limp weight fell and the left side of his face thudded into the hard-packed soil.

"Hurry up," Lisa Stephens said in a misery-laden voice. Blood bubbled over her swollen lower lip. "Get it over with."

Jesse Heller stood behind the jeep with his legs splayed, his face clouded by a grim expression. A murderous look was carved into his features. He watched for a moment as the white-haired man dropped his pants and straddled the naked woman beneath him.

Heller's jaw clenched. His knuckles turned white as his hand fisted tighter around the chain. He felt as if he were looking straight into the past. He wondered if this was the way. . . .

He took a step toward the white-haired man.

10

THE WOMAN'S EYES widened. Her glassy gaze of despair hardened into a look of bewildered fear. She stared up past the white-haired man and looked as if she were watching a ghost rise from the grave. The determination that formed on her battered face froze her would-be rapist; he became as still as a corpse, confusion growing in his eyes.

The chain swished through the air and wrapped around the man's neck like a noose. The man named Pete clawed at the chain, teeth clenched.

With the sudden explosion of rage he felt, Jesse Heller snapped back on the chain, twisting his body in a half pirouette. For a moment he looked like a cowboy roping and hauling in a rambunctious steer, but the violent jerking motion he used seemed to be intended to decapitate the woman's attacker. Heller wrenched the chain-garroted man's head back, lifted him three feet up in the air with a powerful yank and threw him clear off the naked Lisa Stephens. The bare-assed man hurtled past Heller and crunched to the ground, head slamming into the rocky soil.

Heller turned to face the man and watched as the white-haired Pete bounced and reeled into the jeep. There was a loud bang of flesh off metal. The jeep shuddered from the impact.

Pete looked up at Heller, a stunned, frightened, embarrassed look on his face. He grabbed his pants, attempting to hide his nakedness, his wilting cock.

Heller lashed out and drove the chain into the man's exposed lower back.

Pete howled in pain, lurching away. He jumped to his feet, but Heller closed down on him like a shark on bloody chum, flailing the older man's body with another back-thumping strike of heavy metal.

Desperate and humiliated, the man scrabbled away from Heller's immediate range. He snatched his pants up, vaulted to his feet and, enraged, charged Heller like some gored bull.

Heller lassoed the chain around the man's left calf, sweeping his feet out from under him. The white-haired man punched down into the ground, a harsh grunt of pain ripping from his throat. Dust shot out from beneath his sprawled form.

"You son of a bitch!" the white-haired Pete snarled, his ice-blue eyes blazing with hatred.

Heller whipped the chain across the man's face and heard a sickening crack of bone. The blow kicked Pete around on his knees and pointed him toward the jeep.

Pete staggered to his hands and knees, then began to crawl. Blood poured out of his mouth, forming small crimson puddles and turning the dust beneath him black. His pants fell halfway down his butt, exposing a white, quivering, hairy ass.

Heller drove the heel of his boot into the brown crack of the man's rear, hammering his head into the jeep's passenger door. Fury filled the eyes of the man named Hell. He took a step forward, launching a long kick that cracked into the pummeled face as Pete started climbing up off his hands and knees. Pete's mane of white hair seemed to blow out and up off his head as he flipped up in the air and crunched down on the hood of the jeep. The momentum sent him somersaulting backward, his weight denting in the hood before he tumbled off to the other side.

Slowly, Heller walked around the front of the jeep. The long, heavy chain trailed him, rattling over the rocky ground.

He stopped on the front left side of the jeep, stood still and watched as the white-haired man tried standing.

Blood slicked the man's face, wetting red patches in his white locks. He stared at Heller with a distant look, his gaze fading. Heller could almost sense the man's punch-drunk brain demand unconsciousness as he stumbled away from him toward the hill's edge.

The man's pants slipped down to his ankles. Then he tripped over a stone, seemed to teeter backward in slow motion and pitched to the ground. His legs shot up into the air, showing Heller butt cheeks contoured by dust-soiled white underwear. He rolled down the hill out of sight.

Heller moved to the edge of the hill and saw the man flop down the incline. The white-haired man came to rest at the base of the hill, outstretched in a spread-eagled, prone position. Dust rose up along the line of the man's downhill plummet.

Heller turned away, looking disgusted. He checked both men by the jeep for a pulse and found faint but steady heartbeats. He stripped the crew-cut man of the gunbelt, draped it around his waist and buckled it on.

Heller heard the woman's sniffles, and he looked back over the hood of the jeep.

She pulled her jeans on, swaying as if she was going to fall off her feet. But the wall rock behind her supported her as she tugged on her sweater.

Heller turned his gaze off the woman and felt a pang of pity stir inside of him. It was a harsh situation, he knew. He listened to her pull on his leather jacket and wondered how she would handle it.

Silently, he stepped from around the jeep and moved warily toward her.

She choked back her sobs, wiping the blood off her lip with the back of her hand. She hung her head as if ashamed to look at Heller.

The man looked at her punished face as he came to a standstill in front of her. His gaze wandered over the ragged hole where the American-flag patch had been. It had been a memento of his service in Vietnam, and he found himself fighting back his anger. Then he looked at the woman, letting compassion warm his gut and diffuse the violence inside him.

She still didn't look at him.

Awkward, tense moments of silence passed between them.

Heller felt his throat constrict. *Christ, girl,* he thought, *hang in there. I know you've seen hell.*

"Lisa," he said, soft and soothing. He reached out, placed his fingers gently on her chin and lifted her face up. "You gonna be all right?"

She gave him a stiff nod of her head and slumped back against the wall of rock. Tears spilled from her eyes and streamed down her cheeks. Her shoulders trembled. She looked up at Heller. Pain and relief broke through her veil of tears. "I thought you were dead."

Heller showed her a wan smile. "I once had an ex-lover tell me that."

She stared at him, baffled for a moment. She sounded a tentative giggle, then let her stare fall off the man. "Just once?"

A sad half smile crooked his lips. He took his hand off her face and let his arm fall by his side.

The blond woman shoved herself off the rock and stepped forward.

Heller looked surprised when she stretched her arms around him and buried her face into his chest. He brought his arms up and hesitated; he seemed uncertain about something. Her breath felt hot as it brushed up against his face. Heller embraced her. She felt warm, good, tender up against him. He let himself relax, enjoying the closeness of her body, the cushion of her breasts against him.

"How did you find me?"

"Followed their tracks. Sound travels pretty far out in these hills anyway. I saw the dust they trailed. They weren't that far ahead."

"Did you kill them?"

"No. But they'll have a damned good headache for a long time. And they'll have the scars to remember the next time they think about attacking someone."

She pulled her face out of his chest and looked up at him.

"They slapped me around pretty good. But they didn't— Do I look bad?"

Heller saw the gratitude in her eyes. But he also found something else in her gaze, something he hadn't seen in a woman's eyes in a long time. Desire. The image of Julie's face flashed through his mind.

"Just a couple of bruises. But you're as good lookin' as ever."

Heller felt the breeze strike his back. A chill went down his spine. He felt strange all of a sudden and wondered why he'd gotten her involved. He wished now he'd ridden on past her back on that desolate stretch of mountain road.

"What's going to happen to us?" she asked.

For a second Heller seemed pained by her question. He didn't like her searching into his eyes as if she wanted to probe his soul.

"I don't really know."

For a long moment she appeared deep in thought. "You know, I don't really understand you at all. I'm scared. I'm confused. Yet suddenly I feel as if I need to be here. With you. You make me feel stronger. No matter what you might've done before, you're a good man. I sense it. I just don't understand how you could have done what you did, even though I can almost see you doing it. You confuse me, Jesse Heller. I want to know you."

Heller's mouth line sagged. He let out a shallow breath.

She pressed her body into him. "Make love to me. Tonight."

"You're crazy, girl." Heller gazed into her tortured stare.

"Crazy, maybe. Stupid, no. We might not live to see the sun rise."

Heller stepped back and took her by the arm.

"Come on. Let's go," he said in a quiet voice.

Buzz Swann saw the eight black-and-white patrol cruisers a mile in the distance down the interstate. The troopers formed a gauntlet with their vehicles, flanking the road, four cruisers parked on the shoulder of the highway, four along the wide dirt median strip that separated the east-west lanes.

And as he led the pack closer to the cruisers, Swann saw the barrels of pump shotguns thrust into the air, canted across the chest of dark-gray-uniformed troopers with eyes hidden by black sunglasses. Swann knew the troopers were waiting for the outlaws.

Mad Mike cranked on the throttle, shot his Shovelhead out away from the formation. He pulled up beside Swann and pointed at the cruisers. "Now what?" he shouted above the din of chopper engines.

Swann noted the anxious expression on Mad Mike's face but recognized also the glint of blood lust that lurked in the outlaw's dark gaze. A grim look fell over Swann's face. He felt as if he were suddenly disembodied, his mind transported back in time. He had seen that stone-cold-killer look on Mad Mike's face before—in the snake-and-bug-infested rice paddies when AK-47s chattered death from the hills. Slugs rained down on grunts, raw FNGs going down, screaming, flailing in the paddies as the murky water turned dark crimson. Then Swann heard Mad Mike's crazy laughter bellow through his mind and knew Mad Mike could go totally berserk in a firefight. The man had absolutely no regard for his own safety. He always dared fate to take an arm, a leg, his life. It seemed that once the man curled his finger around the trigger of an M-16 semi-automatic rifle, he went *dinky-dau*. Swann saw the brush churned apart with long sprays of 5.56 mm slugs, the thatch-and-bamboo hooches of Vietnamese villages literally being swept away with M-60 and M-79 hellfire, villages suspected of harboring Cong guerrillas decimated, razed by flame throwers that whooshed out great tongues of fire that lapped up everything in their path.

Swann knew how Mad Mike had coped with the experience. He now remembered his words with a chilling clarity, in a voice like a bell chiming in his ears.

"They want me over here to kill somethin'. Fuck it! I'll kill every goddamned fuckin' thing I can."

And he had. Anything that moved. Chickens. Dogs. Mama-sans. Papa-sans.

Swann's mind sank even deeper into the cauldron of terrible memories.

The roar of the Harley choppers behind him reminded Swann of incoming Cobras, of Big Boys and frag grenades ripping apart an LZ that fucking S2s had claimed was secured. Tracers trailing smoke and fire as they split the night. The steady, relentless, deafening *thwump-thwump* of gunships lifting off from the LZ with a crew full of crapped-out boots. Swann had never seen that crapped-out, chickenshit look on Mad Mike's face. That had impressed him. Fearlessness. The jungle had belonged to the guy and he to it. A real intimacy, like a lover's caress, a familiar touch. A crapped-out eighteen-year-old cherry became a hardened man in a hurry. Or he didn't make it. A man learned to think about more than just his own ass. One mistake was all it took to kill a man, to even wipe out an entire platoon. Survival became the only thing that mattered. But Swann remembered how desperate some soldiers seemed to return to the World. And when they'd returned, they had found a land as alien and hostile as the hell zones they'd left behind in the jungle.

The wind lashed at Swann's face, screamed into his ears. His mind returned to the present.

"Just cool out!" he told Mad Mike. "Let me handle this. We got ID. We got gun permits. Spread the word down the line. Cool it. Cooperate."

Mad Mike nodded. "Got it." He eased back on the hand brake and fell away behind Swann. He dropped back into formation and yelled to Turd.

Swann spat off to the side. He let up on the throttle, felt the ice in his guts. He only hoped his men kept their caps screwed on straight.

Buck Morris moved out away from his cruiser into the center of the highway. He lifted the Weatherby Orion Over Under 20 Magnum shotgun, rested the twenty-six-inch barrel on his right shoulder. Two troopers walked behind Morris, flanking the big trooper. One trooper toted a Marlin 120 shotgun, the other a Browning BPS. They pumped the slide actions, a sharp, reassuring sound that seemed to linger in the chill air before the peal of chopper thunder washed over their position. The noise reached an ear-shattering crescendo as the pack of hogs closed down on the cruisers.

Swann slowed his dark blue Panhead.

Through his dark sunglasses, Morris watched the bikers pour between the cruisers. Bikes bunched up on each other as the formation tightened to a slow roll.

Two state troopers, the black muzzles of shotguns aimed skyward, stepped behind the pack and stood unmoving. Another trooper held his arm up. He signaled for the oncoming flow of bikes to stop.

Morris motioned with his left arm for Swann to pull past him and onto the shoulder of the road in front of the last cruiser.

The one-percenters showed the troopers hard, mean-faced expressions. Choppers weaved past Morris and strung out in a line down the shoulder of the highway.

Chaos hacked up a globule of phlegm that he spat out, landing it near a trooper's polished black shoes.

When the last of the bikers was off the road, Morris loudly ordered, ''Shut them down.'' He strode down the line of Sinners.

The flesh under Mad Mike's chin quivered. His breathing shot out through his nose in long, raspy wheezes.

For a moment none of the outlaws moved, seeming to ignore or appear mockingly amused by Morris.

Swann switched off the ignition on his Panhead. Six more engines behind the Sinner leader died. Then the rest of the outlaws followed Swann's cue, silencing their powerful bikes.

A hollow, ringing noise seemed to hover in the air in the moments of tight silence that followed the killing of the last engine. It was a ghostlike sound that faded off into the hills.

Morris shifted his attention to the trooper holding back the traffic. ''Move them on by.''

Sinners snapped down kickstands, leaned bikes over to rest.

Three patrolmen wearing disdainful looks assumed positions near the last of the bikers.

Cars slowly rolled past behind Morris. The big trooper

looked at the bikers' bearded, scraggly faces etched in grim expressions. Morris stepped beside Swann.

The outlaw and the trooper locked gazes for a moment, staring at each other through dark shades.

"The Sinners, huh?" Morris said.

The outlaws focused hard, undivided attention on the big trooper.

"You're under arrest."

Swann shot Morris an angry, startled look. "What?"

"Ahh, man, what's the hassle now?" Turd griped.

"You got something to say, shithead?" Morris rasped. His expression turned dark, his tone ugly with menace.

Turd glowered back at Morris in defiance.

"You're going to tell me there's no helmet law in this state, right?" Morris suggested. "Well, like you, I know that. I also know if I run twenty-eight–twenty-nine on every one of you pukes, I'm liable to find some of these pretty scooters here stolen. But that's not why I'm going to haul every filthy, stinking one of you in," he said. He grabbed at the stock of Mad Mike's M-16, yanked the semi-automatic rifle out of its sheath. "No. You're all under arrest for possession of illegal firearms. And for carrying concealed weapons."

Lobo held up a white piece of paper and waved it at Morris.

Morris walked up to Lobo, looked at the gun permit and scoffed, "You think that piece of paper means something, then you're dumber than you look, creep." He thrust the M-16 at Lobo. "See this? This is Army issue. You need a federal permit to carry one of these. And I seriously doubt," he said, his stony eyes glancing from left to right, up and down the line of bikers, "any of you would ever get a federal permit except in your wildest hallucinations. You didn't think about that, did you? I'm sure some of you were in the war. You got contacts. You have buddies in the National Guard who rip off the armories. Where are those backup units?" he called over his shoulder.

"All available units are spread out in Jeff Davis and Van Horn counties as you ordered, sir," the trooper explained. "They've blocked off all the roads and isolated the area."

"Radio headquarters. I want a van and ten units here within thirty minutes." Morris turned his attention back on the Sinners. "And I forgot to add accessory to murder. Two local citizens were cut down by Uzi submachine guns," he said, nodding at the Israeli subgun strapped around the sissy bar of Bobo's Knucklehead, "just like that one." Morris walked up to Swann, stopped and looked at the biker.

Sweat beads formed on Mad Mike's forehead. A glazed, distant look fell over his eyes. His shoulders began to tremble.

"I suppose you don't know anything about that, do you?" Morris said to Swann.

Swann shrugged and shook his head.

Morris made a clucking sound with his tongue. "I guess they were just wearing your colors for the hell of it, right?" Morris suggested, a caustic edge to his tone.

Swann removed his sunglasses, put them in the back pants pocket of his jeans and looked at Morris with a steady gaze. "Whatever they did, they did on their own, Officer. This is the first I heard about it."

Morris snorted, a contemptuous twist to his lips. "All of you," he said to the bikers, "off the bikes. Hands placed on the top of your heads. You'll be relieved of all your weapons. Your possessions will be searched."

The outlaws grumbled and cursed. Slowly and cautiously, all of the Sinners except Mad Mike and a biker at the rear named Tornado stood.

Mad Mike's eyelids narrowed. A ball of sweat broke from his forehead and rolled down his face. Concerned, Swann looked at Mad Mike.

Tornado sat in the saddle of his '74 Sportster and showed Morris a belligerent look.

"What's the matter with you? You got shit in your ears?" the trooper at the end of the formation growled at Tornado. He jabbed the barrel of his Marlin 120 into the biker's ribs.

Tornado nudged the shotgun barrel away with his elbow. "Watch that, sport."

"You son of a bitch!" The trooper was consumed by an instant blind rage. He whipped the shotgun back and slammed the barrel into the side of the outlaw's head, flipping Tornado off the side of his hog. The trooper pumped the slide action and stepped back as outlaws swung toward him, tense and furious.

"Fucking bastards!" the trooper snarled. "You murdered some good folk! Somebody ought to make you pay."

Swann stood, anger and fear stretching the lines of his mouth.

"Take it easy, Tommy," Morris said. "Just back off."

Tornado shimmied up on his elbows, the heel of his boot hooked on the seat. Blood streamed down the left side of his face. He looked with hate-burned eyes up at the trooper who'd felled him. The Sinner next to Tornado reached down, helping his brother off the ground.

The trooper kept his shotgun trained on the biker. Slowly relaxing the tension in his arms, he lowered the Marlin. He sneered.

"All right, show's over," Morris said. "Let's move it."

The bald-headed Mad Mike stared at the ground in front of him with wide, vacant eyes. He looked disoriented, like a dog in the early stages of rabies.

"Now what the hell's wrong with you?" Morris said to Mad Mike.

"Mike? You all right?" Swann asked.

Mad Mike rose off the seat in silence. He met no one's eyes.

"He's just a little crazy, that's all," Swann told Morris. "The war messed him up pretty bad." Swann pointed toward his head. *"Fugazi."*

Morris seemed unconvinced and kept his tight-lipped expression turned on the bald, chain-wrapped biker for a long moment. Then Morris motioned with his shotgun. "All of you. Move to the front. Away from the bikes."

Swann stepped away from his Panhead slowly and looked back at his bike like a man who feared he might never see a loved one again. He showed Morris a murderous look.

The chains around Mad Mike rattled, a quiet, ominous sound in the heavy silence as the Sinners moved away from their choppers.

11

McCLAN'S MUSCULAR BULK filled the doorway of his jailhouse headquarters. He lifted the Ruger 77 high-powered rifle, cocked the bolt action and snapped a .458 magnum cartridge into the chamber.

"You mean to tell me you don't got that carburetor cleaned yet?" he growled at Compton. "A little dirt, mister, is holding me up from the biggest catch of my life."

Compton tilted the gas can back away from the exposed carburetor and gave the sheriff an irritated look. "More than just a little dirt, Scotty. I got most of it out, but only 'cause I took the whole danged thing off and apart and—"

McClan stepped out of the doorway, slamming the door closed behind him. The glass windowpane rattled. "All right, all right, don't go having a cow."

"Sheriff, why don't you just radio in the highway patrol boys for some help," Dumpy said tentatively. He looked as if he immediately regretted having said it.

Junior towered behind Dumpy. He stared at the sheriff, his fleshy face holding an expectant expression.

A lump of chaw pushed out McClan's right cheek. He launched two streams of brown spit near the feet of his deputies as he let the rifle lower by his side. The sunglasses hid

112

his eyes but not the expression of cold resolve etched into his face. "Let me tell you two something."

Compton continued working with a screwdriver to tighten the bolts on the carburetor cover.

"I don't intend on telling them boys," McClan went on in a patronizing tone, "that I had Jesse Heller roped. Let him get away because his filly got the drop on me."

"But, Sheriff," Junior blurted, "he ain't no common *criminal*. He took on and wiped out all them boys in the Satan's Avengers and Death Stalkers."

McClan put his hands on his hips and pressed the rifle's walnut stock against his side, the barrel pointing toward the ground. He looked at Junior, disgusted. "Junior, you know something? You got more ass than a toilet seat, boy. And if you had nearly as much brains as you do ass, well, you'd be dangerous enough to rip this Jesse Heller's arms off and beat him to death with them. Pride!" he barked all of a sudden. "Goddamn you two—pride, that's what I'm talking about. Don't you got no pride?"

"Is pride worth getting killed for?" Dumpy posed.

McClan's mouth went slack as Compton slammed the hood down on the sheriff's cruiser, snaring the lawman's attention.

"There," the old-timer said. "Ain't promisin' it'll start, but I done the best I could with what I got."

"You done enough, I hope," McClan said, moving off the stoop toward the car.

Dumpy and Junior stood unmoving, looking at the sheriff. "Well, get in."

The sudden beating of a helicopter rotor froze McClan as his hand touched the door handle. The lawmen and Compton looked up almost in unison.

The single-rotor whirlybird swept in from the hills, skimmed the prairie's surface and bore down on the three buildings. Great sheets of dust plumed after the chopper.

The helicopter's landing pads touched soil a dozen yards from the four men. The spinning rotor pushed out a cyclone of dust and filled the area around them with a piercing noise that sounded like the cry of some prehistoric bird.

The marksman opened the door, squeezing through the hole in the bubble-shaped cockpit. Hunched over, he jogged away from the copter.

"Sheriff," he greeted him, "Colonel Morris asked me to check in with you. Wants you to keep him posted. You got anything?"

McClan's mouth opened. He started to shake his head.

"Yeah," Dumpy volunteered, excited. "We seen him! We had him taken."

An incredulous looked formed on the marksman's face. "What?" he shouted over the din of the whipping rotor blade.

"Quiet, Dumpy!" McClan said. "I do the talking around here." Anger and frustration cut his expression. He looked at the police marksman. "Yeah. We had the drop on the son of a bitch, but he got away. His woman, she snuck up behind us with a shotgun."

"When?"

"Been about two hours, maybe," McClan answered.

"So why the hell didn't you radio somebody?"

McClan suppressed his rage. He clenched his jaw, drew a deep breath. Dust blew past him in long, thin wisps. "Damned if I know. I guess I wanted to bring him in myself."

The marksman looked about to snort in disbelief. The gust of the rotor's wind spread his black hair across his face. "This isn't any football game, Sheriff. We're not out here to see who wins. Which direction did they take?"

"West," Junior said.

"South," McClan quickly countered, his voice loud, his tone hard.

"Well, which is it?"

"Southwest," McClan said.

The marksman looked at the three lawmen for a long dubious moment. He shook his head, wheeled and loped for the helicopter.

McClan bared his teeth as Dumpy and Junior turned toward him. "I oughtta kick both your fannies."

Buzz Swann knew it was a bad scene. His hands folded

over his head, he watched the action around him. The black eyes of shotgun muzzles stared the outlaws down as troopers piled confiscated weapons into the trunks of patrol cruisers. Saddlebags and sleeping bags were rifled through, yielding revolvers, knives, machetes. Swann looked at the citizens in their cages as they slowly rolled past the line of captive outlaws. The travelers gaped and pointed through windows as if the Sinners were some strange species of animal behind zoo bars. The Sinner leader felt the anger harden like a lead ball in the pit of his gut.

Sweat dribbled down Bobo's puffy, bearded face. His uplifted arms revealed dozens of tattoos, ranging from coiled snakes and eagles with wings spread over HARLEY-DAVIDSON, to slogans like PAYBACK'S A BITCH. He wore a black undershirt that read MAKE MY DAY.—TRY TO STEAL MY BIKE over the image of a huge revolver poking out from between two Harleys. "Where the hell's Bugger?" he muttered to Swann.

"You got something to say, creep?" the trooper who had cracked his shotgun across Tornado's face growled at Bobo. "Well, just shut it up."

Swann could almost feel Bobo biting back on his rage. But Swann was more worried about Mad Mike next to him. The bald outlaw had a catatonic look about him. He trembled, rattling the chains on his chest. The iron-cross earring jiggled on his left earlobe.

Swann found himself wishing Bugger Jensen would arrive. The Sinner president knew all hell was about to break loose and that if it didn't, the Black Maria would take them all away. And Swann feared once they were taken in it would be a long time before they were back on the road.

"You know, Swann," Morris said, shotgun tucked under his arm as he stepped down the line of outlaws toward the Sinner leader, "I really don't know what in the hell you were thinking about." He dragged out each word in a disgusted, baffled tone. "Riding in a pack. Down a major highway. Armed with weapons not even a law-enforcement officer could get. Dumb, dumb move."

Swann looked at the big trooper and flexed his muscles. The Cobra tattoo on his right biceps seemed to coil as if to strike as the arm muscle popped up. "You dudes are really loving this. Got a lone wof out there snuffing outlaws. Almost makes me think he's got one of them cheap tin pieces pinned to his chest."

"Colonel."

Morris swung his head and looked at the trooper who stood next to a cruiser.

"Eagle One just radioed, sir. They spotted the ten ninety-nine. Apache County."

Morris moved down the line of outlaws, his stride long and swift. "I want all units in the vicinity of Van Horn and Culberson to secure and isolate that area. Double quick. Miller," he said to the trooper at the rear of the prisoner line. "I'm leaving you here in charge with four men. Get these bums into that van when it finally gets here. Then follow us out. Culhane. Cooney. Let's hit it."

Morris hopped into his cruiser. The two troopers opened the doors of the other cruisers and got in. Engines fired up.

The trooper named Miller turned away from the road as the cruisers lunged off the shoulder. Tires grabbed at gravel, spat out funnels of dust. Engines roared. Morris sped off down the interstate, leading the other two cruisers away.

Miller looked at the biker he'd struck down earlier, smiling at Tornado. "Well, well, boys and girls," he said. The heels of his dress shoes rapped on the asphalt as he stepped along in front of the bikers.

A shotgun-wielding trooper stood at the front of the line, another trooper at the end.

Miller wore a scornful expression; he raked the look over the bikers' weird assortment of decaled undershirts, tattoos, long, unkempt hair and beards. He looked like a drill sergeant at inspection. "Big, bad, mean-assed outlaw bikers," he drawled, appearing to enjoy himself immensely. He sneered, looking like a snake poised to sink its fangs into flesh. "Look at this pack of maggoty shit, will you, Bob?" he said to the trooper at the front.

Anger flared in Swann's eyes.

"Why don't we just relax, Tommy?" the trooper said. "Wait on those backup units. No sense in riling these boys."

Miller stared at the trooper. His expression hardened. His lips parted and he looked as if he was on the verge of cursing. Instead, he turned his attention back to the outlaws. "You pukes don't look so mean now, do you?"

The trooper named Bob shook his head and frowned.

"Let me ask you something," Miller continued. "If you're so tough, how come it is you always got to ride in a big, filthy, shit-smellin' pack. You afraid some little old lady's going to bust your balls? Or maybe some big local stud'll whip your butt. Take your woman and fuck her in front of you while you choke on your blood and spit out your teeth. Just look at this shit, Bob. These pukes look set to piss their pants." Miller stopped in front of Mad Mike, resting a gaze on the outlaw with the shaved head. "Look at this guy," he said contemptuously. He stared at the tattoos on the outlaw's beefy arms. "He's got the balls to tattoo his arms with the American flag and a couple of eagles. Like he's some big taxpayer. Or like he's some kind of fighting hero."

"He was."

Miller glared at Swann. The Sinner's soft-spoken, determined-sounding declaration seemed to hit the trooper like a gunshot. "What did you say, boy?"

Swann held Miller's steely gaze. "I said, he was. Three tours of duty in Nam. Got more medals than you could haul off in your cage."

Miller looked at Swann, smug and disbelieving.

"What's the matter?" Swann pressed. "Didn't you hear me? Or maybe you got shit in your ears."

Miller tensed, raising the shotgun several inches, as if to strike Swann. Then he showed Swann and Mad Mike a strange smile. Nodding, he looked at the heavy chains crisscrossing Mad Mike's torso. "War Hero, Hell," he scoffed.

Mad Mike's eyes simmered. His shoulders shuddered. He kept his gaze fixed on the highway, away from Miller, as if he couldn't bear to look at the man.

"Look at him," Miller said in a loud voice. "He can't even look me in the eye. What is he, some kind of chickenshit?" Miller laughed.

No one else did.

A car swished behind Miller in a white blur.

The trooper named Bob sighed, seeming to resign himself to the sadistic badgering.

The other Sinners turned angry eyes toward the trooper, a mass of hostile, angry eyes and hostile expressions. Some of the outlaws slipped their hands off the tops of their heads and lowered their arms.

"I bet you he spent most of his time there just smoking pot or dropping acid. Didn't ya? War hero, my ass. You make me sick to look at you. Take them chains off!" Miller stepped back, pumped the slide action, swung the shotgun up and leveled it on Mad Mike. The trooper seemed possessed by a blind rage. The barrel trembled, inches from Mad Mike's face.

But the bikers with the shaved head just rested a burning gaze on the barrel's black eye, seeming completely unperturbed, a strong, silent statue.

Swann drew rigid, sucked in a breath and held it.

The other troopers looked on, grim faced, concerned. But none of them budged.

Tornado glimpsed the trooper in front of him and watched as the shotgun turned off him. Tornado unclasped his hands, then slid them off his head.

"Christ, Tommy, take it easy, will you?" the trooper implored.

"Take it easy—right, Bob," Miller growled. "Tell that to the folks these bastards always walk over. This damned trash all think they can just ride freer than the wind. Fuck the world, they tell ya. Won't work. Can't raise a family. They rape, murder, peddle dope. And don't you pukes go telling me about charity runs for kids and disabled vets. That's just a bunch of phony crap to try and make yourselves look like something. Shit," he rasped vehemently. "I said to take them chains off, boy, and I meant it. Or I'll blow your head off, so help me God in heaven."

The troopers watched, unmoving.

The bikers tensed.

Miller took a step back, easing the shotgun away from Mad Mike's face.

Swann just stared at the trooper. *The guy's nuts*, fugazi, *cap on backwards*.

Several seconds of cold silence stretched on.

Mad Mike stopped shaking. He held his hard-eyed, distant gaze on the shotgun as if daring the barrel to explode in his face.

A tractor trailer whisked past behind Miller. A great gust of wind brushed out Swann's hair, swept over Mad Mike, seemed to pimple the skin on his shiny dome.

Slowly, the outlaw with the shaved head lifted a hand, wrapped a fist around the chains. He pulled the chains, rattling, over his head.

The line of Sinners riveted flint-eyed, anxious stares on Mad Mike.

There was a dragged-out second of tense quiet.

Mad Mike lowered the chains by his leg and looked Miller square in the eye.

Miller showed the outlaw a vicious, taunting grin. The shotgun started to fall away from Mad Mike's face. "Tough guy, war hero. Now, ain't that just—"

The chains shot up in Mad Mike's fist as if propelled by a grenade charge. Metal cracked up into the breech, splintered wood, shattered the bones in Miller's left hand. The trooper howled in pain, fell away, the shotgun blasting smoke and flame skyward over the heads of the outlaws.

Swann drove a backhand hammer fist into the face of the trooper in front of him, knocking him off his feet as if a carpet had been yanked out from under his shoes. The shotgun clattered to the asphalt. Swann snatched up the Mossberg 5500.

Troopers by the cruisers reached for weapons, but hesitated.

Tornado grabbed the shotgun in the hands of the trooper beside him. The outlaw twisted around, thrust his hips out into the trooper, flipped him over his leg and slung the trooper to the ground. Tornado cocked the slide action, whirling toward the troopers clawing for revolvers. "Freeze!"

They froze.

Within moments heavy bike boots kicked the trooper at Tornado's feet into a bloody, unconscious pulp.

Miller staggered back toward the road. His face carved by
an expression of agony and rage, he held on to the scatter-
gun. He tried to raise the shotgun in his broken, bloodied left
hand.

Mad Mike took a step forward, turned his trunk and swung
out with his right arm. The chains swept around in a long,
craning arc and with a cracking of bone, lifted the trooper up
off his feet. The outlaw with the shaved head spun, a frenzied
look on his face as the trooper Swann had decked clambered
to his feet. The chains whipped out like snakes, coiling
around the trooper's ankle. Mad Mike wrenched the chains.
The trooper thudded on to his back, smacking his head off
the gravel shoulder.

Outlaws pressed in on the cruisers.

"Get the weapons," Swann said. "Lock them in the
trunks. Drive them across the plain and hide these cars in the
hills."

Mad Mike tugged violently at the trooper's chain-wrapped
leg and slid the man toward him. He brought his boot up,
hammered his heel down into the trooper's mouth, splintered
teeth and jawbone and pounded the lawman's skull into the
road.

"Hurry it up!" Swann ordered, outlaws reaching into the
trunks to reclaim weapons. "Let's get the hell out of here."

Swann looked up and down the highway and found the
lanes empty of traffic at the moment. But he knew the road
wouldn't stay that way for long. He turned and watched as
Mad Mike stepped down the highway, the chains hanging
from his big fist, rattling along the road as they trailed him.
Swann glimpsed the two bodies of the state troopers outstretched in the road. He looked at Mad Mike as the outlaw
with the shaved head drew near. Swann saw the cold-killer
glint in his dark eyes, the splotch of blood his boot heel left
on the asphalt.

Swann heard the first Sinner chopper rev back to life.

12

*T*HE DUST ROSE like a pall of smoke, funneled up over the peaks of jagged hills and vanished against the dark clouds that skirted the late afternoon horizon. The sky threatened rain. Boiling cloud belts folding high over the plateau as Jesse Heller guided his seventy-four-cubic-inch iron belt toward the pillars of dust. Cautious, wary of the rugged, uneven, rock-studded surface, he kept his chopper in second gear. As he neared the plateau's outer limits, he heard the faint grind of diesel engines in the distance. He braked his chopper on the lip of the plateau.

Heller stared down at the valley. Hills surrounded the deep basin like a fortress, as if the earth had been scooped out with thousands of gigantic steam shovels. The rock quarry reached even deeper into the valley, like a pit dug into the bottom of a volcano. Heller watched, listening to the clank of conveyer belts lifting massive boulders that would be ground up into gravel. A green, stagnant lake stretched away from the sheer cliff faces to the south. Diesel engines strained against fifteen-ton loads and gears meshed as the twin-axle dump trucks rolled out of the gate and up the long, winding road that snaked between the hills.

Lisa Stephens looked over Heller's shoulder; she kept her arms entwined around the man's midsection and her chin rested on his shoulder. Her mouth was bruised, swollen from the beating she had suffered, but strength and determination had returned to her eyes like a rekindled fire. She looked at Heller.

"What are you thinking about?"

Heller searched the land, the dark, ominous-looking hills to the north of the plateau. The engine vibrated between his legs like a racehorse anxious to break out of the starting gate. He was concerned about his bike. The engine had run hot and hard, day in and day out for more than a week. It had jarred across countless miles of tortuous, rut-cut terrain, and dust and dirt caked bent chrome pipes, dented outer primary cover now turned black by exhaust and engine heat. The powerful engine idled in choppy sputters. Plugs needed changing. The carburetor should be cleaned, even rebuilt, he knew. If he cracked the cam and blew a gasket because of the rough ride along the desert floor, then they were in serious trouble. But at least now he had retrieved all of his weapons, the money and the dynamite.

"Thinking ahead some, that's all," Heller told her. "We have to stop for the night. Find a hole up in those hills. This isn't a trail bike, and I hate like hell to have to be so hard on her. I bust something on her, we might have to get out of here in one of those diesel rigs. Besides," he said, looking at the dozen dump trucks that rolled through the quarry, spewing dust behind fat double tires, "we might have to get out of this place in one of them anyway. The bike's too easy to spot."

"You're going to leave it?"

A thin, sad smile cut Heller's lips. "I'd hate to do that." He patted the gas tank. "We've been down a lot of roads together." He turned his head sideways. "How's your mouth?"

She showed him a smile, leaned up, kissed him on the cheek.

Heller lifted an eyebrow. A grin ghosted his lips. Yesterday, he remembered, he was just a bike bum to her. But things had happened, life-threatening events had changed them, he reflected. He accepted this, accepted whatever would happen to them, between them. Perhaps, he thought, it's only in desperation, when someone's ass is on the chopping block, that a man gets to really know another human being.

Heller slipped the chopper into gear, let out the clutch and wheeled around. He felt the warmth of her body as she nestled against his backside.

Dumpy lowered the binoculars away from his eyes and pointed toward the hills to the north of the patrol cruiser. "There, Sheriff. Don't that look like Butch Peterson's jeep?"

McClan peered through the windshield and saw the black Renegade parked on the hill perhaps a mile away. "Sure does. I wonder what that's all about?" he said suspiciously. As the cruiser's wheels jarred over a rut, he saw Junior kicked forward against the front seat. McClan shot the deputy a baleful look.

A trail of dust followed the patrol cruiser as it jounced across the plain. The car stopped at the foot of the hill in front of the outstretched, unmoving frame of the white-haired Pete. McClan shut off the engine as he took in the scene: the body at the hill's bottom, the two bodies stretched out near the jeep at the top of the hill.

Mackie stirred from in back of the jeep. He groaned and pried open his eyelids, prodding the purple lump on his forehead. He grimaced, lifted his back off the ground and braced himself on an elbow.

The three lawmen stepped out of the cruiser, shutting the doors as dust thinned around them. McClan looked at Pete and moved toward the man who had his pants draped down around his ankles.

The sheriff bent at the knees. He rolled the man over on his back and winced when he saw the battered, bloodied, dust-smeared face. He felt the neck for a pulse. "Grab my canteen, Junior."

"Jesus," Dumpy breathed, gazing at the man's pulped features. The deputy looked as if he was going to retch.

"Him, he ain't," McClan said, disgusted.

Mackie clambered to his feet, his shoulders slumped, his knees shaking. He stared down the hill at McClan. A sheepish expression formed on the big man's face.

"What the hell happened here, Mackie?" McClan asked gruffly.

Junior walked up behind the sheriff. He hesitated at the sight of the punished face beneath McClan. His flabby face seemed to wither up into a look of horror.

McClan grabbed the canteen out of Junior's hand. He uncapped the canteen, sloshed water over Pete's face, washed away some of the blood and dirt and shook the man's shoulders. McClan looked up at Mackie. "Well?"

A muffled moan sounded from Pete's throat.

McClan stood, nudging the white-haired man's ribs.

"There was this biker," Mackie started, tentative and embarrassed.

McClan handed Junior the canteen. "Go on. I'm listening to you. What about this biker?"

"Well, he, uh . . . you see, he, uh, jumped us. Surprised us."

McClan looked at the still form of Butch Peterson. The sheriff nodded, pursed his lips, looked doubtful. "Why did he jump you?"

Mackie shrugged, a pathetic, helpless expression on his face. "Hell, I don't know. He had a woman with him, and Pete there, well, he, uh, made some crack. The biker chain-whipped us. Just chain-whipped us!"

"Uh-huh." McClan glanced down at Pete, who groaned and made a feeble attempt to move his arm. "Want me to tell you what it looks like to me, Mackie? Looks to me like Pete Starbers here made more than just some crack. Looks to me like you three tried this dude on for size, tried to have a good time with his woman. Looks like this time you pushed just a little too hard. And it sure does look like you pushed the wrong dude, buddy-boy. If I had a camera I'd take a picture of this. Take it down to the lodge and hang it over the bar. Big, bad-ass Mr. Joe Mackie and his buddies. The terror of Apache County. Shit!"

Butch Peterson rolled onto his side. He opened his eyes, showing McClan a swollen, lopsided, blood-smeared face. He let out a sharp cry of pain as he pushed himself up off the ground. He staggered like a drunk, then fell back into the jeep. He cupped his jaw in the palms of his hands, his eyes shut, his face screwed up in agony.

"All right," Mackie growled. "We fucked with the guy, but he damn near killed us. He almost strangled me to death. He's some real bike trash. No telling all he's done. You gonna do something about it?"

McClan nodded. "Yeah. I'm going to do something."

"What?"

"I'm going to take your jeep, because my cruiser won't hold up in this kind of country. Official police business."

"The hell you are!"

"The hell you say," McClan rasped. "I bet I come up there and check that M-16 of yours, I find a few rounds missing. You always were a trigger-happy bastard, Mackie. You and those no-account bums. I should've run you out of this county long ago. I know you sons of a bitches ride around this desert killing all the wildlife. Do it here 'cause you know better than to try that a little farther north with the park police. If I ever took a slug out of one of them mule deers I find on occasion, I bet it'd be a five fifty-six slug. This time I'm letting it go, since you three finally got what was coming to you.

"Now, you just shut your hole and give me that rig or I will haul your asses in and lock the three of you up. Pete and Butch might not like having their faces mend behind bars. Looks to me like they're going to be spending some time over at County General." McClan vented a soft snort. "Least there they'll be safe."

Butch Peterson squatted on his haunches, his face pressed into his hands.

Mackie looked at his comrades. He spat noisily. "I'm gonna get me this bastard, McClan. I'll break his neck for this. Pete and Butch ain't gonna just let it slide neither."

McClan snickered, shaking his head. He squished a line of tobacco juice from his mouth, splashing a rock in brown muck. "That I'd really enjoy seeing, tough guy. You know who kicked your bad asses today? Well, I'll tell you so's maybe you'll think again. Jesse Heller."

"What's a Jesse Heller?"

"The dude that killed all those bikers last week. By himself. That's who you bucked up against. Yeah, bad-ass, you are damned lucky he didn't kill you.''

A heavy silence fell over Mackie. He looked away from the sheriff, a dark expression clouding his face.

Butch looked up out of his hands and gazed down at Mc-Clan.

A smirk started to crease McClan's face as he stared up at the silent Mackie. ''That's just what I thought you'd say.''

The brown Ford cruised west on Interstate 10 at a steady fifty-five miles per hour. Mountains flanked the long, empty stretch of highway, dwarfing the lone vehicle.

The radio transmitter-receiver beneath the dashboard, beside Garrett's leg crackled with the voice of Buck Morris.

''Ground One to all units in the vicinity of Allamore. This is a code two. Proceed at once. Apache County. Ten ninety-nine. Subject sighted in Apache. All units, repeat, all units proceed at once. Acknowledge. Over.''

''This is Ground Nine to Ground One. Ten four on the code two, Buck. Over.''

''Ground Five . . .''

Garrett turned down the radio's volume and swung his head. Excitement seemed to sharpen his gaze as he looked at Dudley. ''They got him, Dud.''

The map folded out across the dashboard crinkled in Dudley's big hands as he smoothed out the edges. ''Highway Fifty-four. We still have a good thirty, thirty-five miles. Another fifty, sixty to Apache.''

''You still wondering if it was worth it, Dud? Hell, they'll have Heller in cuffs by the time we get there.'' Garrett's voice sounded torn between relief and disappointment.

Dudley looked at his partner for a moment, concerned. They had driven hard, nonstop since leaving Dallas late that morning. They were monitored in on the Mutual Aid frequency. The ten codes had been coming over the airwaves like the staccato of machine-gun fire for the past hour.

Garrett's raw enthusiasm had mounted into an obsession following the first code 10-99.

Dudley searched Garrett's face.

The gray-haired detective had a look in his eyes that the Marines termed "the thousand-yard stare."

"Wes? Wes? You all right?"

Dudley's voice shook Garrett loose from his dark, private mood.

"Huh, yeah. Sorry."

Dudley let out a long breath through his nose. He rumpled the map together, laying it on the seat between him and Garrett.

"Listen, Dud. Thanks for coming along."

"Ah, don't mention it."

"No, I mean it. I never told you this before, but it's damned good to have you as a friend and as a partner. You've got a good wife too, the best. She stands by you, tries to understand a cop's life. I envy you for that." Garrett locked gazes with his partner for a long moment.

An awkward silence followed. Dudley broke the eye contact.

"Yeah, well, I don't think she'll be so sympathetic next time out. Not that there's going to be a next time. It's a good thing I had some sick time coming. I'm afraid Allison's going to be crawling all over us anyway."

"Fuck him, Dud. Sorry, I know that doesn't do you much good now. But I'm just about fed up with this shit. Maybe I'll just hand in my badge when we get back."

"And do what?"

Garrett shrugged. He seemed pleased with himself for a second, as if he had something all figured out. "Get a PI's license. Maybe set up shop out in Fort Worth somewhere. I need a change, Dud. I think I really need something where I can call my own shots for once. I'm burned out, Dud. Homicide works a real killer, no pun intended. It's a soul killer, big man. After a while, seeing what the human animal can do just eats away at your guts until you can't really separate the good guys from the bad guys. Everyone becomes crud. Including yourself. It's just time for a change, or I might lose my mind."

Dudley looked away from Garrett, out the window. He felt a chill tap his spine, as if he didn't really know his partner at all. Yet he feared that Garrett was right. He thought about his two children, his wife. He looked at the desolation that reached out from the highway. He longed for Sheila's warm embrace.

''Ground Run Twelve. En route north on Fifty-Four. . . .''

The brown Ford whisked along, a lone vehicle down the interstate.

=== 13 ===

JESSE HELLER SENT the Harley chopper up the long, low rise toward the sheer walls of limestone rock. Dust spewed out in the wake of the iron beast, but Heller heard something else besides the growl of the powerful engine between his legs: a faint, bleating sound—but a sound that loomed just beyond the peaks like a swarm of insects.

He topped the rise, braked the bike. The ravine stretched out in front of him, spining a wide but boulder-studded trail that cut through the towering rock sheets. Funnel-shaped holes riddled the base of these walls of rock, walls that had been tunneled out by some prehistoric ocean.

Heller listened, staring up at the peaks.

"What is it?" Lisa asked.

"Helicopter."

Heller popped the clutch out and shot down into the ravine. There wasn't a second to waste. He feared that from the air they would be as easy to spot as a herd of caribou moving across a snowy plain. Silently, he cursed the trail of dust that thinned too slowly behind his bike.

Heller cut a sharp, dangerous swath between the rocks. He headed straight for the dark maw of a cavern and sent the chopper into the mouth of the cave. A roiling brown dust ball swept across the opening as the fugitive couple vanished into the darkness.

The helicopter soared between the knife-edged ridges and swept down between the rock walls.

Heller wheeled the chopper around, back tread spitting out rock and dust like a fan.

Frenzied bats screeched through the cave as the din of Heller's Harley boomed like cannon fire down the cavern.

The woman's face twisted. She cried as hundreds of black, furry creatures fluttered in wild zigzag paths over her head.

Heller slid the chopper along the wall. The ripe stench of bat guano was cloying in his nose. Shrill bat cries filled the cave with ear-piercing reverberations.

Heller killed the engine and waited.

Lisa meshed her body against Heller's backside, slouched low in the buddy seat as flocks of bats spiraled around her, swarming into the cave's mouth. She winced as bat bodies thudded off the cave walls.

Heller looked out into the gorge. He slitted his eyelids to cracks as a huge wave of dust blasted into the cave. The whir of the copter's rotor seemed to swell his brain with a terrible whining.

Lisa sank lower in the seat. She shielded her face against the rush of wind, dust and noise, and hid from the crazed flight of bats.

A moment later the whirlybird blurred past the cave's opening. Dust hanging thick and brown blotted out the murky evening light, turning the cave pitch-black for several seconds.

Heller hopped off the saddle and stepped into the opening. Dust pouring down over him, he stood there, watching as the helicopter pulled up and streaked out of the gorge.

Jesse Heller knew that there were times when a man didn't question a lucky break. Rather, he had seen that it was misfortune that always made a man question the order of things. Now was one of those times when he didn't question the luck of the draw as the whirlybird disappeared beyond the saw-toothed peaks.

He turned and looked back at Lisa. She seemed unnerved,

hunched low in the saddle. She glanced around several times, looking as if she expected the horde of bats to forage on her flesh.

"I hate bats," she said. "If there's one thing I can't stand, it's bats."

The silence in the cave thickened. Heller listened, hearing the distant fluttering of wings, the quiet squeaking as the bats retreated into the black recesses.

"You leave them alone, they leave you alone." He flashed her a wry smile. "Besides. They'll keep the bugs off you."

She frowned. "Funny."

"You be all right here by yourself?"

Her gaze widened. "Why? Where are you going?"

"Just to get some brush, some wood for a fire. Trust me. They won't bother you now."

She appeared dubious.

Heller looked at her for a moment, then left the cave.

She looked around. A dark expression came over her face. She frowned, slid off the seat and folded her arms across the front of the jacket. Slowly, she walked to the front of the cave, her head craned sideways to look behind her.

McClan lowered the binoculars from his eyes and lifted his elbows off the hood of the jeep. He watched while the helicopter flew east past the rock quarry, over the plateau a mile and a half north of his hilltop vantage point. The Ruger 77 high-powered rifle lay across the jeep's hood, within McClan's reach.

Junior and Dumpy flanked the sheriff. Both deputies wore perplexed expressions. They looked as if they wished they were somewhere else.

The binoculars came away from the marksman's eyes.

"What do you got?" the pilot asked, his voice loud but muted by the noise of the whirling rotor.

"It's that dumb-ass McClan and his two deputies. There's a rifle on the hood of that jeep. He's just standing there, watching us and these hills. Like he knows something."

"You think our man's down there in that ravine?"

"I don't know. Might be. I'm going to call it in."

"Listen, Mike. I can't stay up here any longer. I've got to refuel."

"Right." The marksman reached for the radio mike.

"Think he's seen us?" Dumpy asked.

"Sure he's seen us. No big deal," McClan said. "What he didn't see was Mackie and his tough boys. And what he couldn't follow up there was them bike tracks."

"But, Sheriff," Junior declared, "them tracks didn't get us here. Least not all the way here."

"Junior, let me tell you something." McClan looked over his shoulder at his fat deputy and scowled. "That run-in Heller had with Mackie cost him some time. Especially since he had to backtrack to get the girl, then whip their butts."

"If you believe what they told us," Dumpy said.

"Why shouldn't I believe them?" McClan growled. "I would've locked their stinking carcasses up and thrown the key away. And they knew it.

"Listen, knotheads. We covered a whole lot more ground quicker than he could've by having to baby that hog of his. And unlike you two, he ain't stupid. He knows he's as wide open on that bike as a mama's legs for a train." McClan looked back at the ravine, toward the towering, sheer cliff faces. "He's down there all right, mark my words. And there's only one way out of there—this way. If I don't miss my guess, he'll be going for one of those diesel rigs in that quarry. He'll just have to find a way down there first."

"So what do you want us to do?" Dumpy asked sourly.

"You? I don't want neither one of you to do a damned thing except what you've been doing—holding on to your butts. He's down there, dammit, and I intend to stay right here. And when he rears his ugly outlaw head . . ."

McClan fisted the Ruger's stock, hefted the rifle in his hands and cocked the bolt action. He showed his deputies a cold smile.

Fear flickered over Dumpy's face.

"It's bye-bye, one Mr. Badass Jesse Heller."

The Sinners rolled their choppers into the arroyo. Dust boiled over the outlaws, folding over the members at the end of the formation. Sinners amassed their bikes in front of Swann as he wheeled around to face his troops. The leader killed his Panhead's engine.

Bugger Jensen guided his Sportster beside Swann and flipped off the ignition. The rest of the outlaws shut down their bikes, but the engine noise seemed to linger and bounce off the sides of the arroyo.

Swann looked over the horde of expectant faces. Dust choked his lungs, and he coughed to unclog his windpipe. He looked at his troops and didn't like what he saw on several faces—fear, anxiety. He knew he had to regroup his men, reassure them, regain control over them.

To Swann, Mad Mike still looked as crazy in the eyes as he had when he'd chain-whipped and stomped the two state troopers. Swann worried about Mad Mike.

"Okay. We've had a setback—a problem called the highway patrol," Swann said, his expression grim, his gaze dark. "We all expected to hassle with them, so getting pulled over didn't come as any big surprise. What surprised me is that they wanted to haul us in so bad. All right, we're in a jam, but let's keep our caps screwed on straight. They fucked with the Sinners. And nobody does that. Stuffing them in a trunk with bullets in their heads puts the whole scene in a different way. But we knew this might happen before we rode out. I just hope there's no second-guessing. If anyone's having second thoughts, speak up now."

Silence met Swann.

Jensen raked a cold gaze over the troops.

Swann nodded. "Good. Because this Heller bastard poses a real problem, not only to us, but to outlaw brothers everywhere. All of us know the pigs won't do a damned thing to this dude if they catch him. They're making the son of a bitch out to be some kind of hero now.

"Silvers and Burton went down, bit the dust because they were always squabbling between each other. They couldn't get their shit together. They weren't tight like a brotherhood should be, like we are. But like them we need the bread that the coke and the doo-gee and the pot bring in.

"Y'all knew the score with those college punks. Heller's got Stilson's old lady. If the Man gets to them, Heller just might use her to plea bargain and save himself. She squawks about the college punks we snuffed, we're as good as dead anyway. Getting to her is every bit as important as snuffing Heller.

"A lot of us were over in the Nam. We know how a scene can get *fugazi* quick. We got us the number ten right now— the worst. But you dudes been in tighter jams than this, shown real class. There ain't no cherries here. You're all hardcore biking motherfuckers. So keep in mind we might have to take out some more troopers to get to Heller and the bitch. Unless we get to them first.

"We're out here in the middle of no-man's-land. Nowhere. We leave no witnesses. We ditch the weapons when it's over. We boogie in the wind for a while, lay low. We did it before when we snuffed those two cops down in Houston. Mexico's been good to us. It's real pretty down there. All the señoritas love us too."

"Pig man's radio said the bastard was up north, around Apache," Lobo said. "That's some wild desert country, Buzz. Be hard on our scooters." He shook his head, appearing regretful. "I sure hate to bust up on Lou-Lou Belle here."

Swann nodded. "None of you love your scoots more than me. But if we have to chase them through those hills and even into the Guadalupe, we'll do it. I've been behind the wall. I don't intend on ever doing time again. I'll hold on to my freedom at any cost, do whatever it takes. And right now it's going to take some killing. Stilson's old lady has to go. Listen. We're all in this together. Deep together. There's just no turning back.

"We ride out, fifty hard guns ready to rip the shit out of anything that stands between us and Heller and her. We've all had blood on our hands before. It's just a question of having bigger balls this time."

Swann sat on his chopper, silent for long moments. He let his stare wander over his troops, searching their faces. His eyes appeared to smolder with some dark emotion. He seemed possessed as he sat rigid in the saddle.

"From here on out," he said in a low, ominous voice, "snuff anyone who tries to stop us. If the bastard's in these hills, then we're going to be the first and the last ones to see him alive." Swann paused, extended his left arm, clenched his fist. "Outlaws forever—forever outlaws."

The Sinners raised balled fists and chanted, "OUTLAWS FOREVER—FOREVER OUTLAWS."

Mad Mike's eyes glazed over with a distant stare. "Fucking right on." The chains crisscrossed over his chest rattled as he jumped down on his Shovelhead's kick starter.

A fire burned in Swann's eyes. In the back of his mind, he wondered if this might be their last run. A blood run, he knew, was the final, desperate act of a gang holding on to its freedom. And it usually landed outlaws behind bars, or dead. But Swann had left himself with no choice.

"Fuck it," the Sinners' leader muttered, his boot plunging down on the Panhead's kick starter.

"Did you love her?"

Heller, squatted on his haunches, hands clasped between his thighs, stared into the flames, his eyes reflecting the wavering orange glow from the fire he'd built. Shadows skirted across the rough face of the rock wall behind him. He appeared deep in thought, and it took him a long moment before he seemed to hear her question. He listened to the crackling flames as he looked at Lisa. She sat opposite him on the other side of the fire, her hands dug into the pockets of the leather jacket.

"Yeah. I did." A bone in his knee cracked as he stood. The holstered revolver was a heavy weight on his leg.

"Do you think about her a lot?"

Heller looked down at her, searching her face. He found himself irritated by her question and wanted to know why she had asked. But as he gazed at the softness in her eyes, he felt the tension in his gut melt away. He showed her a sad, strange half smile and turned away. "I try not to," he answered. "Most of the time it's all just some blur—the memories, that is. Until I see a picture of her. Or unless something reminds me. Are you hungry?'' he asked suddenly, wishing to change the subject.

''No.''

''Good,'' he said. ''I'm getting tired of pork and beans myself.'' He moved into the cave's opening, staring out at the ravine, his back to the woman.

She sat in silence for a moment, her attention riveted on the flames. She looked as if she was mesmerized by the fire. Finally she looked toward Heller as he leaned his shoulder against the rock.

''Are we going to make it, Jesse?''

Heller drew a breath, his eyelids narrowing. All of a sudden, he felt an emptiness inside of him. ''I don't know. Right now everybody in this part of the world wants a chunk of us. And up to now, things have just been too quiet. It was like this over there.'' He looked up at the sky, watched the bubbling mass of dark clouds high above the peaks. ''Like the calm before the storm. You could feel them out there somewhere. Just watching. Waiting. Closing, creeping in.'' He faced her and slumped back against the rock wall. ''That's why we should leave here. They're getting close. They'll be here very soon.

''It'll be dark in a few hours. We'll go down to the quarry. I'll wire a truck. The bike has to go.''

''We could head south, try to make it into New Mexico. They'd never find us there.''

Heller didn't like the hopeful ring in her voice. He felt pain touch him, but he nodded, smiled and stared back out at the walls of the gorge.

''What's the matter?'' she asked.

''You don't seem to understand. They won't let it rest—the Sinners are scared of you, what you know. They'll keep hunting for you until they get you. Now that I'm in the picture, it only makes it worse. For you.''

''We can run.''

''But not forever. We'd be looking over our shoulders the rest of our lives. No,'' he said grimly. ''I started something I have to finish. I started it the day I pulled a trigger on an outlaw biker. I have to meet the Sinners head on. Finish this score with them.''

''But it's a score I started.''

Heller shook his head. ''You haven't killed any of them. If I know the way these guys think, they aren't far behind, even now. They'll fight and trip all over the Man to get to you. To even the score with me. So, you see, it's not really so cut and dry that all we have to do is keep on running. There'll always be other outlaw bikers. There'll always be a gun coming after me. No. Right now, somewhere out here in this Christ-forsaken hellhole, I've got to finish what started back at that diner. The Sinners will be one less bunch I'll have to look over my shoulder for.''

She dropped her gaze off Heller and stared into the fire. Her mouth line sagged. Her eyes misted.

Heller shifted his attention, looking out at the mouth of the ravine. He let his mind go blank, draining himself of any feeling—for himself, for the world, for the insanity that had claimed his life the day he'd returned from Vietnam to discover his life shattered. The torture inside of him lay dormant, but he knew that was only temporary, a false sense of security.

The woman's touch surprised him, jolted him out of the state he'd lulled himself into. He turned his head and found her staring up at him. Her eyes seemed like liquid pools of pain and desire. It was a strange look she showed him, but the warmth of her hands on his arms made him suddenly forget why they were there, what had happened to them.

''You misunderstood me,'' she said in a whispery voice. ''That's not what I meant when I asked you if we were going to make it.''

He held her gaze for a moment and felt the tension ebb out of his muscles as if his body were a deflating balloon. He felt some part of him that had been dead for so long come to life. She made him feel free, good, warm, alive. The harsh memories, the pain vanished inside of him like puffs of smoke in a breeze.

Their lips touched, brushed, soft as butterflies' wings.

Heller let the warmth stoke in his belly, felt it spread like smoldering ash into his loins.

Gently, he took her in his arms and lowered her to the ground. He felt the fire's heat against his arms as he molded the curves of her flesh, soft and warm in his hands. He pressed his lips to her mouth, rested his bulge on her thigh, felt her tongue darting into his mouth. Her fingers moved through his hair with a scratching sound. She cupped the back of his head, pulling him to her. She lifted a leg and squeezed him between her thighs.

Jesse Heller wanted the moment to last, wanted the fire he felt burn inside to go on forever as he slipped his hands inside the jacket and palmed her breasts.

14

*H*E PULLED UP his corduroys and tugged up the zipper on his pants. The muscles in his arms, chest and shoulders looked chiseled from stone as the firelight flickered over his bared torso. He ran a hand through his sweat-dampened hair, slicking the short, wet strands back from his glistening forehead.

"Why are you getting dressed?"

Heller looked down at Lisa. She was snuggled in the bedroll, her face pressed into his jacket. Long tangles of sweaty blond hair fell over her face as she looked up at him.

His gaze wandered over the word she had tattooed in red letters on her shoulder: LOVE. He forced himself to look away from the creamy white smoothness of her arms and shoulders as she wriggled her hands beneath the jacket. He felt a pang of regret stab into him.

Heller reflected back on their coupling, remembered the passion she'd awakened in him, how her touch, her wet mouth had ignited a fierce desire in him. There had been a tenderness yet a hunger in her yearning, as if some inner pain had driven her, as if she had known all along that their coupling would never be shared again. He couldn't help but recall how it used to be with Julie. They had only shared each other twice, but it was something he would never, could never, forget, as if a part of her lived on inside him. They had been the first for each other. And now he heard his mind saying, *blissful union*. That was how he'd always referred to their lovemaking. Julie had liked that.

"Jesse?"

Heller crouched, dropping down on his rump. He looked at her, reached his hand out and brushed the hair back off her face. He massaged her neck.

She moaned and opened her eyes, a sleepy, peaceful look on her face. "That feels good."

He stopped rubbing her neck.

"Don't stop. Why don't you lie here with me awhile?"

Heller slipped his socks on, pulled on his bike boots. "I'm going to have to leave you soon, Lisa."

Her eyes widened. "What? Why?"

"I want you to turn yourself in. I don't want you to get hurt or killed because of this."

She sprang up, propping herself up on an elbow and pulling the bedroll over her breasts. "No. I'm staying with you."

"No, you're not."

"Yes, I am. We've gone this far together. I'd be really crazy to try to make it on my own now. What with every cop and outlaw in this state after me. Right?"

Heller looked at her for a moment in silence.

"Whatever happened to the idea of the outlaws finding a way of getting to me if I turned myself in to the police?" she said adamantly. "Remember that? Why the sudden change of heart?"

Heller started to stand, but she put a hand on his shoulder to stop him. He looked at her and said, "Get dressed."

"Does that mean I ride with you?"

His gaze hardened. "That means get dressed."

She frowned, hurt by his sharp tone. "Why are you contradicting what you said earlier?"

Heller let a breath rasp out of his nose and felt his muscles tense. But his look softened. He knew she was right. "Maybe it's because I like you." He looked away from her.

A smile tugged at the corners of her mouth. She sat up,

naked, and knelt back on her haunches. She slipped her arms around him.

Heller reached up to place a hand on her arm.

"What's changed your mind about me?" she asked, her voice suggestive, as soft as a cat's purr.

"Who said I ever changed my mind about you?" A smile ghosted onto his lips. "You're as beautiful as when I first saw you." A wry grin cocked his mouth. "And you're kind of tough too. Now let's get out of here," he said in a quiet voice, gently unclasping her hands.

The trooper looked up over the hood of his cruiser, radio mike in his hand. "Colonel. Units four, six, eight and ten still don't acknowledge. Wagon unit reports there's no sign of the bikers or the officers and their vehicles at the detention sight."

Morris' expression darkened.

"No more available units are in the area, Colonel."

Morris turned his gaze from the officer, rested his attention on Mackie, scoured the pummeled faces of the big man's two comrades. Behind Morris two cruisers rolled across the plain toward the tiny town.

Morris tried to steel his nerves with a deep breath as he felt the tension tighten a knot in his gut. Eagle One had radioed him forty-five minutes ago to give him the exact location of McClan and his deputies. Morris knew the sheriff as a stubborn, proud man. So it came as no surprise to him that McClan had taken off on a glory hunt for Jesse Heller. Particularly if Heller had shown McClan up. Morris had seen many small-town Texas sheriffs like McClan. Once their pride was tarnished or their authority challenged, they became almost fanatical, going after their quarry like some rampaging rhino. Morris had to get Heller first, before anyone else got injured, maimed or killed. He didn't believe Heller was a psychopathic killer, but he knew the man was dangerous. Morris didn't have to look any farther than the battered ruins of the three faces in front of him to determine that.

"Keep trying, Pinson," Morris called over his shoulder.

"Contact the EC van. If those bikers are loose, I want the Rangers in on this. Quick. Then radio Eagle One. I want that copter refueled and out here double quick."

A dozen troopers waited outside their cruisers, fidgeting, hands draped over the butts of holstered revolvers.

The two cruisers stopped and parked outside the line of patrol cars.

"You said McClan left how long ago?"

Mackie shrugged. "Hell, it's been a good two hours now. Headed west toward the rock quarry."

"All right. Get yourself over to the hospital. I'll get back to you later."

"I sure hope you nail this son of a bitch."

Morris stared at Mackie. He felt a chill go down his spine at the sight of the cold hatred he found in the big man's eyes. A war-honed gut instinct nagged Morris, warned him that the manhunt was getting set to explode right back on him and his men.

"Because if you don't," Mackie continued, "I won't rest until I track him down and make him pay for what he done to us."

"Don't be shooting off your mouth and saying things you might regret later," Morris warned. "You got enough problems now as it stands. I plan to check your story out." Morris saw Mackie's expression tighten and the trooper waited a second, as if tempting the big man to say something, then he wheeled and strode toward his cruiser. "Let's move it out."

Buzz Swann saw the curling plumes of dust and made out the shapes of fifteen black-and-white highway patrol cruisers rolling across the plain. The Sinner leader led the formation off the road and up a rise in the desert floor. He topped the rise, braking his Panhead. There he stared at the line of cruisers more than two miles in the distance, the cars veiled, vanishing behind a mountainous wall of dust.

The choppers halted. They flanked Swann, stringing out along the crest of the incline. Outlaws revved engines as if eager to give chase after the cruisers. Rifle and shotgun stocks jutted skyward out of brown and black leather scabbards. M-16s and Uzis hung from the shoulders of two dozen Sinners. Exhaust and dust mingled into black-brown balls that shot out from behind pipes.

Bobo and Lobo looked each other, faces etched in tense expressions.

Mad Mike stiffened his back, sat up straight in the saddle. His gaze burned on the edge of rage.

Smoky adjusted his Nazi helmet, pushed it up straight on his head. He spat.

Swann looked at Jensen and motioned with his arms toward the hills to the south. "Cut them off. We'll go north, pinch them in on the other side of those hills. Half your men come up from behind. Shoot to kill. Take no prisoners. The pissing around's over."

A twisted grin showed on Mad Mike's face.

Bugger Jensen nodded.

Smoky spat.

The Sinners gunned their engines with a massive, thunderous sound. Choppers poured down the incline.

A cloud of dust the size of a tidal wave billowed, unfolding behind the Sinners.

The black Harley 74 roared over the rise and shot out of the gorge on a blast of dust. Heller headed the iron beast across the plateau.

Lisa leaned up, her arms wrapped around his stomach. "We're in this together, right? You won't go turning me in to the police, will you?"

Heller turned his head and felt the tires jounce over stone. He smiled, nodded and faced front. "We're in this together."

He felt good about the woman, recalled their lovemaking.

He should have been hardened against their threatened future, alert to the grim fate he knew lay ahead, but he momentarily chose to forget about the dangers.

He heard the crack of the rifle a moment before the bullet whined off a slab of rock several feet to the side of the chopper. He shot a startled gaze toward the hills and found the

Renegade jeep; it was barely outlined against the dark sky, black on black.

Heller hit the throttle.

The woman lurched backward against the forward surge.

McClan pumped the bolt action and chambered another .458 magnum round. He swung the rifle up, sighting through the scope.

Dumpy threw his weight into McClan and jarred the sheriff. The rifle exploded a round. Dumpy wrestled with McClan, struggling to take the rifle away.

"You can't just shoot them!"

McClan wrenched the rifle out of his deputy's grasp with one forceful yank. He slammed his palm into Dumpy's chest, shoving him back. Rage contorted McClan's features. "What the hell's the matter with you? What the hell are you doing?"

Dumpy froze. He stood back, petrified.

"I ain't going to kill them!" McClan bellowed. "I was aiming for his tire, damn you!" He pried his gaze off his terrified deputy and saw Heller streaking across the plateau toward the jagged hills to the east. "Damn. Now he's getting away." McClan snatched open the driver's door and tossed the rifle behind the seat. "Get in!"

The radio crackled between Garrett and Dudley.

"Affirmative on that ten ninety-nine, Ground One. Due west of Apache. Backup units from Jeff Davis en route. Estimated time of arrival . . ."

"Look," Dudley said, thrusting his arm out to point past Garrett.

Garrett stepped on the brake to slow the cruiser.

"Tell them to hurry it up. Code ten thirty-nine. Ground One. Over."

Sweat beads glistened on Garrett's forehead as he stared at the long line of dust a mile out on the desert plain. His breath came in short rasps. The veins on his hands stood out, throbbing as he threw the wheel hard to the left. "Bikers. Looks like those Sinners to me, big man."

Dudley's jaw slackened. He muttered a curse, reached over the seat and grabbed a 12-gauge pump shotgun.

Garrett bounced the front end down on the rugged, rocky desert floor.

Lisa twisted around on the buddy seat, wind sweeping her hair across her face.

The Harley bounded through a rut.

Heller gnashed his teeth and felt the bone-jarring jolt rattle through his bones.

The black Renegade bounced like a huge ball across the plain, tires spraying out sheets of dust.

"It's that crazy sheriff!" she yelled.

"How do you know?"

"The hat!"

Heller chanced a look behind him and saw the jeep bearing down less than a hundred yards away, cutting the gap quickly.

Heller kicked the big bike into third gear.

"I got you now, boy! I got you now!"

Junior's face bashed against the back of McClan's seat as the jeep pounded through a hole, tires thumping over humped rock.

Dumpy stared through the windshield, his eyes wide, his hands braced against the dashboard.

McClan sounded a harsh, raucous laugh. His eyes seemed to strain from their sockets with a look of murderous intent.

Heller hit the foot of the rise, tires slamming down with a wrenching impact. Shock waves shot up the front forks, threatened to rip the bars out of his hands.

The woman cried out in alarm as she was bounced upward, off the saddle, but she landed on the seat, her hands digging into Heller's side like steel clamps.

Ahead of them the rise appeared to blend into the sky. Heller topped the crest, shot out over the edge. The chopper soared down the incline like a seagull skimming a calm ocean surface. Heller lifted his butt off the seat and tensed himself for the crash he knew was coming, for the slope was too steep, too treacherous. Everything became an instant blur in his vision, the sky a gray circle in his eyes.

The front wheel hammered off the slope. Heller felt the woman's nails cut into his flesh as the back end banged down and twisted around. Then the uncontrolled speed and momentum flung them off the bike.

In one desperate attempt to keep the chopper upright, Heller threw his body backward into the uphill grade, against the point of contact, and turned the bike.

Lisa flipped off the side and rolled back into the hill.

The chopper whipped sideways, kicking Heller out of the seat and sending him over the high side into a headlong dive down the hill. Instinctively, he lunged away from the chopper and thudded into the hill on his side. He began his end-over-end tumble and felt the wind driven from his lungs as if a sledgehammer had bashed into his guts. As the dust clogged his throat and stones punched into his ribs and back, stripping the skin off his arms and neck, the world spun before his eyes in a hazy pirouette of sky and land and rock. His skull missed cracking open against large, protruding rocks by inches. He rolled, tumbling head over heels. The Ruger magnum flew from his holster and clattered off rock, following his plummet.

Finally he stopped, smacking his elbows off stone at the base of the hill. Pain tore through him. He gritted his teeth and looked up. He saw the woman fold up onto her hands and knees, heard her utter a groan. His chopper lay in a tangled heap a dozen yards down the incline from her.

Then the jeep sailed over the crest. The vehicle slammed down, the frame shuddering against the impact.

Lisa shot a fear-filled look toward the jeep as its front end bore down on her less than twenty feet away.

Heller snatched up his revolver, triggered two lightning rounds.

The Renegade's front tires blew.

Heller saw the panic cut into McClan's face. He cursed the sheriff for his recklessness and watched the jeep careen away from the woman, out of control. The jeep's flattened treads reeled up over rock.

Heller thumbed back the hammer on the Ruger.

The jeep flipped over, smashing down on the driver's side. The rig rolled across the slope at an angle.

Heller heard the roof collapse, glass exploding. He looked up and saw the woman pick herself up off the ground.

"You all right?"

She looked at Heller and nodded. A line of blood ran down the side of her face, a dark crimson streak that parted the plastered dust on her cheek.

Metal groaned. The jeep dipped down on its left front end, lifted up into the air in a weird, slow-motion stand.

Heller bit back against the waves of agony that coursed through him. He raised himself up on an elbow.

The jeep rolled over once more, onto its caved-in roof, and settled on its wheels. Dust thinned around the rig.

Thick silence stretched across the slope.

Heller looked up the rise. He found oil running out of the chopper's engine, spilling into the dust. He cursed to himself, knowing the bike was shot. He felt as if a part of him had just been hacked out with a dull knife.

Gun in hand, Heller clambered to his feet. He shifted his attention to the jeep's crumpled-in side door and saw the movements of three men inside the vehicle. He heard a moan, a curse. A sea of glass slivers lay across the jeep's dented hood. Heller stood unmoving for a long moment, numb with pain, caked with dust. For a second the sound of gunfire didn't register in his mind. Then he heard the staccato barking of machine guns. He swung his head and stared out across the plain.

Heller felt his heart sink into the pit of his stomach. His gaze widened in disbelief, his expression like that of a man able to look inside his mind and see his worst nightmare unfold.

Jesse Heller watched the Sinners converge on the patrol cruisers and surround the cars from every side and angle. The sounds of rapid-fire machine guns, death screams and shattered glass stretched across the plain, striking at Heller. He stood there like a man drifting on wreckage at sea who's just spotted a dorsal fin knifing toward him through the placid waters.

15

OUTLAWS CIRCLED, CUTTING off the patrol cruisers, using their choppers like cowboys on horseback rounding up a stampeding herd.

Except the Sinners were turning the plain into a slaughter field, soaking the dust red with blood. Windshields imploded on shocked faces instantly obliterated by 9mm and 5.56mm sprays. Horns blared as bullet-shredded corpses slumped down over steering wheels. Unmanned cruisers rolled aimlessly across the desert floor. Several outlaw bikers went down screaming as cruiser tires churned them up, mashed their flesh into the metal of their bikes. Two lawmen used their vehicles like battering rams, plunging head-on into outlaw charges, scattering pieces of iron and severed limbs.

But the Sinners held the final, brutal edge. They used automatic and semi-automatic weapons fire to corral the cars and force the lawmen from their cruisers.

"Get out of here!" Jesse Heller yelled up at the woman as he ran up the incline toward his downed chopper.

Lisa stood as if frozen. Her mouth opened and she started to shake her head in protest.

Anger flared in Heller's eyes. "Get the hell out of here. Save your ass."

She didn't move.

148

"Goddamn you! Run!" he screamed as he stopped beside his bike.

Fear and hurt seemed to glaze her eyes, but she stood, calm and unmoving. "No. Not without you."

Heller clenched his jaw. He looked at her for a stretched second, then tore his gaze away and returned his hard-eyed attention to the massacre. His hand fisted around the walnut stock of the Weatherby. He slid the powerful rifle from its sheath and cocked the bolt action. He swung the rifle up and knelt on his right knee, left leg extended down the hill, his weight shifted back toward the incline. He listened to the boom of shotguns, the chatter of M-16s, watched the outlaws hustle lawmen from their cruisers. Dust swirled across the scene of the lopsided battle, cloaking the movements of men behind a thin gray curtain. A lone cruiser with its front and back windshields blown out trailed across the plain, then slowed.

Heller sighted through the scope.

The woman's expression stretched taut.

The man named Hell adjusted the scope for the two hundred yards distance. He lined the cross hairs up on a yellow, upside-down Jesus, drawing a steady bead on the outlaw's obscene logo. Heller waited a long moment for the dust to clear, listening to the sharp tones of voices barking out orders and threats, to the thunder of choppers. The Sinners, too consumed by their blood lust, hadn't spotted him. Surprise belonged to Heller. Why they had attacked the troopers, he wasn't certain, but he was sure it had something to do with him.

Jesse Heller wouldn't stand by and idly watch the slaughter of good men.

Still the Sinners hadn't seen him.

Heller's finger curled around the trigger and squeezed. The rifle bucked in his hands as it cannoned a .460 magnum slug.

And his own war raged on, perhaps for the last time.

The bullet tunneled out a gaping hole in Turd's back, spraying a gory cloudburst of blood, flesh and cloth. The impact lifted the Sinner off his feet and kicked him onto the hood of a cruiser. He crumpled, falling facedown into a bed of glass shards.

The peal of the rifle's boom washed over the Sinners and the lawmen. Heads snapped up and around. Men froze.

Smoky stared at the blood that drenched his colors. He looked at the corpse of Turd spread-eagled across the hood. "What the . . ."

M-16 in hand, Swann stiffened, paralyzed in the act of dragging a bloodied Buck Morris from his cruiser. The trooper looked up at Swann, eyes filmed over by blood, sweat and pain.

Swann let go of Morris and stepped away from the car.

Slowly, Heller stood. He pumped the bolt action, ejecting the spent casing. "That Swann? The blonde?" he asked the woman.

Lisa stood off to Heller's side and nodded. "That's him."

"Next shot fired," Heller called down, "I'll drop you where you stand, Swann."

Thunder boomed from a coal-black sky. A gust of wind swept across the plain as the storm clouds gathered high above the mangled bodies strewn around the remaining squad cars.

Mad Mike bared his teeth, fingers nervously tracing the length of his M-16's barrel. Sweat glistened on his smooth skull.

"Hold it," Swann ordered, motioning with his arm as Lobo and several Sinners aimed rifles toward Heller.

Tornado tossed a trooper to the ground behind Swann.

McClan flung open the driver's door of the jeep and leaned out, showing a bruised, blood-smeared face. He looked dazed.

"Out of the jeep, Sheriff," Heller said, his voice taut. "You and your deputies. Toss the guns out first. Step to the front of the jeep so I can see you."

McClan glared at Heller defiantly.

"It's a standoff right now, Sheriff. You go playing hero again, they might kill every one of those troopers. You want that on your conscience?"

"Send the chick down here, Heller!" Swann bellowed.

Lisa froze, rigid with tension.

Heller cupped his hand under the rifle barrel. Blood ran down his forearm from a deep gash in his elbow, plastering the dirt to his skin.

"You send her down here," Swann yelled. "If you don't, I kill the rest of these lawmen."

Heller worked his jaw. His nostrils flared, his eyelids narrowed. A beaded line of sweat broke out on his forehead, trickling down his grim, dirt-grimed visage.

"Don't do it, Heller!" Morris shouted. "They all know they're finished. Stall them. Help's on the way."

Someone plunged a boot into Morris' gut. The trooper grunted, a harsh, guttural belch.

"Buzz!"

Swann turned.

Several choppers rolled up behind the cruisers.

"Who the hell are those guys?" Swann growled.

"Probably the help that's on the way," Smoky suggested, his tone caustic.

Heller tried to make out the newcomers. He felt fear and anger cut deep into him. He watched as the Sinners shoved Garrett and Dudley along, nudging the two detectives with shotgun barrels. Outlaws gathered up the nine remaining patrolmen and stood them in a line beyond the cruisers.

"Good thing you said for us to fall behind," Bugger Jensen said, braking his Sportster between two cruisers. "I didn't see nobody else."

"Heller!" Garrett shouted. "Don't turn yourself over to these animals. Gut it out."

Swann snatched Garrett and thrust the tip of his M-16 under the gray-haired cop's chin, forcing his head up and back. Garrett's eyes widened.

Dudley felled a biker with a sweeping right roundhouse to the jaw, but rifle butts chopped across his head, dropping the big detective to his knees as he charged Swann.

"Animal?" Swann rasped. "All right, wise asshole. Heller!"

McClan and his deputies stepped to the front of the jeep, holsters empty, revolvers discarded in the dirt beside the front tires of the jeep.

Junior stood on wobbly legs. Blood pasted the hair to the back of his neck.

Dumpy looked from Heller to the armed Sinners out on the plain. Fear shadowed his face. He swallowed.

McClan staggered for a moment, his shoulders drooping. Pain and defeat carved his expression.

"Your buddy here gets it first, Heller, if that bitch isn't down here in two minutes."

Dead silence fell over the plain. No one moved.

A peal of thunder sounded from beyond the hills.

Heller tightened his grip on the rifle.

"You gonna just stand there, boy?" McClan rasped. "It's you they want. You gonna just let that vermin kill all those men? Good men. Law officers. Men with families."

Heller glimpsed McClan, dismay flickering through his eyes. He looked out at the outlaws, at Garrett, and felt a terrible pain rise up, choking him as he thought about the two Dallas detectives.

You dumb sons of bitches, he thought, feeling a terrible weariness settle over him. *What in the fuck do you think you're doing here? Throwing your asses away for this. Dumb, Dumb, Dumb. Don't you know we're all going to die out here in this godforsaken asshole of the world?*

Bobo swung his Uzi toward Morris. "Touch that radio, man, you're out of this world."

Morris froze, his hand inches from the radio mike.

Swann pushed Garrett away from him. "Walk out there."

Garret hesitated, his gaze fixed on the M-16 pointed at him. "Move!"

Heller tensed. He put the rifle down and grabbed the Uzi. He pulled three spare clips from his saddlebag and slipped them inside his gunbelt. "Swann! You kill that man, I'll drop as many of you as I can. You want me, you come and get me. But not here. You let them go. All of them."

"I want the woman too."

Heller paused. His face hardened to a cold mask. "Then you're going to have to fight for her."

Swann stiffened.

Garrett walked away from the bikers, toward Heller.

"Throw everything in the jeep," Heller told the woman. "Start it up. Take it to the top, behind us."

"What are you going to do?"

"Just do it. Don't ask questions. *Now*."

She moved to the chopper.

Heller and Garrett looked at each other. The detective stopped a hundred yards from the rise.

Heller searched the cop's face and saw behind it a tired, beaten man. "Why did you come here, Garrett?" He kept his tone low, but his words carried with sharp clarity across the plain. "You had to make it personal, didn't you? Now here I am, trying to keep you from getting killed just so you can come and hunt me down."

Garrett showed Heller an odd, self-deprecating frown. "You should've listened to me that day in my office, Heller. But you had to go and do it, didn't you? Now can you see what I was talking about? This insanity you started just keeps spreading. And it will keep on spreading because they won't let it alone until you're dead. This vengeance hunt of yours, Heller—it wasn't worth the lives of those troopers, was it?"

"You spout a lot of questions, Garrett. I don't think either one of us has those kinds of answers. Besides, they didn't know I was out here."

"What's that?" Garrett asked.

Lisa, saddlebag and shotgun gathered in her arms, walked down the incline toward the jeep.

"They were after her," Heller said. "She saw them murder two college kids over drugs. And you and I both know how crazy it would've been for her to turn herself in for protective custody."

Swann looked on, anxious. "Fuck you, Heller. What's it going to be? You and her, or the lives of these lawmen?"

McClan watched Lisa as she set the saddlebag and shotgun on the floor of the jeep. "Your boyfriend's making a big mistake, honey. Why don't you just turn around and talk him into giving himself up to those bikers. It's him they want."

She looked at the sheriff.

"If you're in trouble, the law will take care of you," he added.

She showed McClan a look of disdain, turned and faced Heller.

"Start it up," Heller said, shifting his attention back to Swann.

The woman hopped into the jeep and shut the door.

"We'll meet, Swann. But on my terms."

"What terms?"

"I say we blast the motherfucker!" Jensen snarled.

"Quiet!" Swann growled.

"Kill those radios, Swann," Heller said, hearing the jeep's engine cough to life and noticing in his peripheral vision the black exhaust puff out of the tailpipe. "The tires too." His expression darkened. "I don't want anyone following us. It's just me and you. And a whole lot of Sinners."

Swann seemed to think about something for a moment. His jaw jutted. He nodded several times. "All right. Do what he says. We can come back and take care of them later."

"You sure that's the smart thing to do, Buzz?" Jensen asked.

"No, I'm not sure, but we've got no choice," Swann rasped. "We've got to take care of this or we're all fucked."

The jeep rolled up the rise and parked behind Heller.

Heller bent down to pick up the Weatherby. He looked back at Garrett. "Wish me luck, Garrett?"

Garrett snorted and shook his head, a resigned look in his eyes. "Good luck, you crazy asshole."

"Sheriff," Junior bleated.

"Shut it up, Junior."

"I hope it never has to come down to you or me, Garrett," Heller said, his tone heavy with weariness and sorrow. "Or Dudley."

"In all honesty, Heller, I was hoping I could have saved your ass."

"Then say a prayer," the man named Hell said as he turned to head up the incline.

Garrett expelled a long breath and watched Heller as he opened the driver's door.

Heller turned and heard the gunfire; he saw the outlaws blasting out the tires on the cruisers, ripping out radio mikes.

They seemed possessed, consumed by their wanton destructiveness, like savages set free after years in a cage. Heller saw a big Sinner with a shaved head take a chain from around his chest and cave in the few remaining windshields.

Thunder rumbled.

The sky darkened behind Jesse Heller.

=16=

*H*ELLER STEERED THE jeep into the fold in the hills and bounced the rig out onto the road that led to the quarry. The flattened front tires made a squishing sound over the asphalt, forcing Heller to fight the wheel with every jolt and turn. Wind blew glass slivers off the jeep's hood and through the blasted opening where the windshield had been. Air lashed his face. Glass chinks pelted his skin.

"You just stay down when the bullets start flying, you hear me?"

She looked at him and acknowledged his hard-toned order with a nod.

He didn't know how far behind they were, but he knew the rugged terrain would slow them up and put the bikers at least a mile or more behind. The jeep's side-view and rear-view mirrors had been crushed by the tumble down the hill. The canvas roof hung in jagged strips around their heads.

"What are you going to do? How can you take on all of them by yourself?"

"I'm not going to do it all by myself."

The road dipped down at a steep descent toward the quarry.

Heller saw three diesel rigs parked by the large green pool. "We're in luck."

"What?"

"We're taking one of those rigs. Think you can handle the dynamite?"

She threw him a strange, questioning look.

Giant walls of sheer rock loomed like sentinels over the battered jeep.

Swann knew he had lost control of the situation as he led the outlaw pack off the desert, up a rise and onto the road. He felt the fear inside of him edge toward panic. And the only way to regain control of himself, to rid himself and the others of any fear was to eliminate the causes.

Heller.

Lisa Stephens.

The state troopers they had left behind.

Over in Vietnam Swann had seen how things could go from bad to worse to a nightmarish hell, when men would start dropping dead in their tracks from the bullets of unseen snipers. He recalled the fear over in Nam, a clawing, unshakable fear that lived inside a man, day and night.

That's how Swann felt now.

But Swann knew they would kill Heller. The son of a bitch was only one man, one lone-wolf bastard who'd just gotten lucky, suicide lucky against a careless, reckless gang of disorganized misfits that had been the Satan's Avengers.

Swann looked at his *segundo*, Bugger Jensen, saw a hard, grim, determined look on Jensen's face. Behind the *segundo* rode Mad Mike, as fearless and as crazy in the eyes as Swann had ever seen him.

The Sinner leader faced front and felt a steely reassurance. These were the best guns, the meanest, most brutal fighters and outlaws he had ever seen. In any man's army. Swann knew the Sinners were the meanest sons of bitches to ever saddle a hog.

But the fear lay like a cold, wet rag in his gut.

The scene was *fugazi*.

Still he knew Heller was one dead lone-wolf bastard.

The road descended into the valley. The hills seemed to darken under the onrushing storm clouds.

The wind screamed at the Sinners.

The jeep crashed through the flimsy wood-and-wire gate.
Heller sluiced the rig around and shuddered to a halt in front
of the trailer.

He hopped out of the jeep. "Put everything in one of those
rigs." He bounded up the steps to the trailer door.

Lisa slid out the jeep's door, saddlebag slung over her
shoulder.

Heller drew the Ruger, shot off the lock, opened the door
and went inside the trailer. He saw a small refrigerator, three
chairs, a file cabinet and a desk. He opened the desk drawers,
rifling through folders and papers. He found the six separate
keys in the bottom drawer.

"Damn," he muttered, then fisted all six keys.

He delved into his pants pocket, withdrew the wad of cash
and peeled off six one-thousand-dollar bills. He stuffed them
in the drawer and slid the drawer shut.

As he moved toward the door, he heard the coughing grind
of a diesel engine turning over. He stood in the doorway and
saw the woman in the cab of a diesel, wires in her hands.

The engine fired up. She pressed on the gas pedal, turned
and looked at Heller. "Bo showed me how to do this once.
Rip a couple of wires from under the dash," she said, shrug-
ging. "Put the ends together—zap. You want me to drive?"

Heller tossed the keys on the desk. He leaped over the ban-
ister and hit the ground feet first, absorbing the shock with
his knees.

"How did you get so handy? Slide over," he said as he
climbed up into the cab and slammed the door shut. "You're
a nutball, girl," he said. He looked at her and felt a strange
flash of sadness warm his belly. Then he ground the clutch
into first gear and wheeled the rig around, grim faced. The
Uzi and three bundles of dynamite lay on the seat between
him and the woman. The barrels of the Weatherby and 12-
gauge leaned against the edge of the seat, pointed toward the
roof of the cab.

Heller threw the rig into second gear and felt the stick shift
quiver in his hand. The drive shaft strained as he sent the rig

climbing up the incline out of the quarry. He was grateful for the truck's empty bed.

"Jesse?"

Heller looked at her and found fear shadowing her gaze. He broke her stare and lurched the rig into third gear as the incline petered out.

The dump truck headed down a long, winding stretch of road between towering cliff faces.

"Those are twenty-second fuses. Light one when I tell you. Count to ten, then out the window. Got it?"

She let out a pent-up breath and clutched one of the dynamite bundles.

Heller looked into the side-view mirror. In the shimmying glass, he saw the Sinners pop over the rise less than a mile behind. The leaders at the head of the formation vanished for several moments down the incline as the road dipped into a swale. Then the lead choppers soared over the crest of the incline past the quarry.

Heller knew they'd seen him. Sweat broke out on his forehead. He felt his heart hammer against his ribs, felt the ice chill his guts.

He looked out through the windshield and followed the bend out onto a long, straight stretch of road. He noted the dirt shoulders reaching away from the two-lane road, then dropping off for a steep ravine. Ahead, the sky seemed to scrape the peaks of the hills, black clouds surging over the saw-toothed caps. Heller listened to the wind lash against the sides of the truck.

He downshifted, braked and turned the rig around.

The truck stopped, to sit in the middle of the road.

Heller gripped the steering wheel, his knuckles stark white. A drop of sweat fell off his jaw. He felt the engine vibrate through the cab and under the seat, as if the engine were some great beast fighting to free itself from its cage. He looked at Lisa and tried to put the fear out of his mind—his fear for her safety.

"You hit the floor when I tell you. Cover your head. Don't get up, even if I leave the cab. You understand?"

She stared at him uncomprehendingly.

"Understand?"

She nodded stiffly, her gaze brimming with worry.

Heller let out a breath. He pushed the stick shift into first gear and eased out on the clutch.

The truck rolled on smoothly, then lunged into second gear. The engine growled as Heller cranked the rig into third, demanding speed.

"Come on, you sons of bitches," he muttered, tight-lipped. "Okay. Light it!"

She fumbled around in the jacket pocket.

"Come on," he urged as he shot the truck forward into fourth gear. He heard a match scratch and flare to life.

The fuse sizzled.

Heller looked at the speedometer—fifty—and watched as it climbed to sixty. He felt the cab tremble, heard the engine roar in protest.

Where the hell are you? he thought.

Time stretched in the cab. Heller listened to the burning fuse as he counted off ten seconds in his mind.

The truck bore down, rumbling toward the bend, a great shuddering metal beast.

The Sinner pack rounded the curve.

Heller glimpsed the woman. She seemed paralyzed. "Out!"

He faced front, looking through the windshield as Swann led the outlaw pack thundering around the bend. Choppers swung up, racing straight on toward the speeding dump truck.

The woman tossed the bundle out the window, sending it bouncing along the asphalt behind the truck.

Heller read the terror on Swann's face, saw the panic. Then the lead choppers became a blur in Heller's vision as bikes spit off to the sides of his murderous charge.

Swann's Panhead tumbled, banging off the road.

Jensen crushed on the Sportster's brakes, the bike snaking around sideways, sliding out from under him.

Mad Mike careened.

Dozens of choppers made a desperate last-second swiping turn.

Heller plowed into the heart of the formation. Bodies,

rending metal catapulted off the rig, cartwheeled into the air, over the roof of the truck. Wreckage exploded. Broken corpses sailed over the hood, and choppers crumpled on impact with the front of the rig.

The windshield imploded on Heller's face under the crushing, screeching tide of metal. He covered his face with his forearm as glass shards shattered against his head. The woman dropped to the floorboard, the cab shaking as if the tires had bounced over mine blasts.

Then Heller realized it was the tires crunching up flesh and iron.

Smoky's chopper sluiced out from under him. His Nazi helmet skimmed across the road like a cannonball.

Tornado tumbled to the road. His face appeared naked with horror an instant before he slid under the truck's front tires, his body instantly ground up into a blood-spewing, twisted sack. Bits and pieces of metal trailed the speeding rig. Wheels spat out warped junk.

Smoky shot out over the lip of the shoulder. He screamed as he followed the plummet of his chopper down into the ravine.

Mad Mike skated on his back down the road, rolling and rolling.

M-16s clattered down the asphalt behind jouncing, spinning bikes.

Heller ground the gears down and mashed his foot on the brakes. "Light another one!"

He looked at the side-view mirror, into the cracked glass. Violently, he threw the wheel left, meshed gears and swiveled the rig around.

The first bundle of dynamite blew. A roiling orange fireball seared across the road, sucked up and hurtled bikers and bikes skyward. Delayed blasts shook the asphalt like an earthquake, kicking men and metal sideways. Severed limbs crested orange-red tongues of fire.

Swann clambered to his feet to look at the flaming ruins of his Panhead. He cursed as he scooped up a Mossberg 5500 shotgun and cocked the slide action when the shock waves of an explosion floored him.

Fire crackled, and licked over the choppers, igniting pools of gas. Explosions puked choppers apart.

Heller shoved the truck into second gear.

Lobo groaned and rolled onto his side. He clawed for an M-16. Terror widened his eyes. The rig crushed him, snapping his back.

Mad Mike triggered his M-16.

Heller flinched and ducked as 5.56mm slugs peppered the hood, whining off metal and through the cab, punching out glass.

Lisa thrust the second bundle of dynamite at Heller. The fuse had almost burned down when Heller grabbed the bundle and flung it out the window.

Mad Mike dove out of the truck's path.

A dozen outlaws, all in various degrees of pain and injury, crawled or ran across the flaming road. Hands scrabbled for weapons.

Heller threw the truck into a long skid. White smoke spewed out behind squealing rubber. The rig lurched down the road. Heller turned the vehicle sideways, fisted his Uzi and grabbed the last bundle of dynamite.

A hail of lead ricocheted off the truck.

"Stay down!" He lunged across the seat.

"Aaaaaaaahhh!!!" Mad Mike roared, legs splayed, M-16 bucking in his hands.

Blood slicked Swann's face. He stood as Jensen, Bobo, Cheese Nuts, Pisser and other outlaws fired, pressing toward the truck with blazing weapons. Swann saw the second bundle of dynamite sizzling less than ten feet away from the leader's face. His eyes bulged as the last quarter inch of fuse burned. He felt the curse explode in his chest, but the scream lodged in his throat never emerged as TNT ripped an ear-shattering ball of smoke and flames through the outlaws. Wreckage razored across the road. Chunks of asphalt drilled into Sinners.

Jensen and Bobo slumped to their knees with debris speared into their chests and stomachs.

Heller slipped from the cab against the tremendous con-

cussion. The last dynamite bundle fell from his grasp and
thunked to the road.

Heller looked beneath the truck's frame and saw a dozen
Sinners charge his position, shotguns and M-16s spitting
flaming tongues. But Heller, crouched on his knees, un-
leashed the Uzi. Sinners howled in agony as 9mm lead shredded their legs out from under them.

Mad Mike crabbed to the shoulder of the road. There he
lay utterly still. His eyes stayed open wide.

Lisa threw open the door.

"Stay in there!" Heller snarled, slamming the door on her.

Outlaws stood on wobbly, blood-drenched legs.

Heller stepped around the front of the rig. He cradled the
Uzi, a dirt-and-blood-smeared, steely-eyed wraith, looking
like something that had just walked out of the bowels of hell.

Thunder rumbled across the sky.

Choppers blew apart.

Heller smelled the burning gas, the torched flesh. He triggered a long burst, stitching Sinners with long sweeps of the
chattering muzzle.

The woman lifted her head inside the cab, showing her
face.

Bullets spat off the road around Heller, tattooed the sides
of the truck. Heller stood, emptying the thirty-round clip into
the eye of the bullet storm. He felt burning sensations tear
across his shoulder and the outside of his thigh, but he ignored the pain. He released the empty clip, slammed another
one into the magazine and saw movement behind the sheet
of flames. Heller, legs apart, face twisted in agony, fed off
his fear of death like a shark chewing off a man's bloodied
arm as he parted the fires with long, raking sprays.

Fire masked the few surviving Sinners. But Heller fired,
saw shadowy figures whirl, spin death jigs.

For long moments Heller listened to the roar of the fire.
He straightened, wisps of acrid white smoke curling up from
the Uzi. He looked at the bodies strewn across the road, mutilated, mangled lumps twisted and slashed amid a sea of
wreckage.

Heller lowered the Israeli subgun by his side. Blood dripped off his hand.

The clouds opened on a long peal of thunder. Rain cascaded, spattering the asphalt and seeming to kiss the flaming debris.

Heller limped down the road toward the flames, the boiling black clouds of oily smoke. He prodded the opened flesh along the outside of his right thigh and felt the warm stickiness of blood wash down his leg. But the bullet had only sheared off a good slice of skin.

As Heller stood outside the circle of carnage, he felt a numbness settle over him. He drew a deep breath and froze as he caught movement to his side. He swung his head and saw the chain swinging toward his face. Ducking, he heard the metal swish an inch past his ear. Heller lunged up and started to swing the Uzi around, but the biker with the shaved head moved like a panther leaping out of the night. The chain coiled around Heller's leg. Pain shot through his body as metal thudded into bone, wrapped around his calf.

Mad Mike yanked, hauling Heller's legs out from under him.

Heller's head cracked off the asphalt. The Uzi slipped from his hands. The Ruger magnum slid from his holster and bounced away. Rain slashing his face, Heller felt nausea bubble in his guts, saw a white haze in his eyes.

Mad Mike wrenched the chain off Heller's leg. An animallike growl sounded from his throat. The chain swung up over his head.

As Heller rolled, he saw the chain plummet for his face. He threw himself clear and heard the heavy metal strike the road with a rattling thud, felt the vibration of metal pounding off asphalt beneath his back like some slithering reptile.

Mad Mike drew the chain back.

Heller vaulted to his feet and dropped his head as the chain arced over his skull.

The crazed Sinner whipped the chain back, entwining Heller's leg, and swept him off his feet.

Heller flipped onto his stomach and stretched his hand out for the Ruger magnum. Fear shot through him as he felt the

Sinner haul on the chain, trying to pull him away from the revolver. But Heller snagged the gun's butt and scraped the stainless-steel barrel over the pavement.

A howl ripped the air. The Sinner with the shaved head lifted his boot.

Thunder boomed. Lightning cracked across the sky.

Heller swung the magnum up and thumbed back the hammer.

The boot plunged toward Heller's face.

The revolver cannoned a .44 slug, the gun bucking in Heller's fist. He twisted his head and felt a boot heel slam off the back of his skull.

Mad Mike toppled and thudded into the road on his back. The chain slapped the rain-slicked pavement beside the Sinner's headless body.

Heller leaned up, his arms shaking. He gritted his teeth, feeling the pain knife white-hot through his limbs. He let the rain pelt his face for several long moments.

Finally Heller lifted himself to his feet, stood and holstered the Ruger magnum. He felt the adrenaline rush hot through his blood, heard his heart pounding in his ears. Everything whirled, hazy in his sight like a white fog. He felt the bile burn like acid in his gut. He took a step on rubbery legs. His head spun from the dizzy sickness spreading into his chest.

Heller turned and limped toward the truck.

His head cleared with each step. He listened to the driving rain, to the faint, fading crackle of fire. Then, as he neared the truck, he saw the door, the hood of the rig riddled with countless bullet holes. He limped up to the vehicle on wooden legs, his face grim.

A heavy silence seemed to surround the truck. Heller felt the fear fight with the queasiness in his stomach.

"Lisa? Lisa!"

Heller hopped around to the passenger side, teeth gnashing against waves of agony. He grabbed the door handle, twisted and flung open the door.

He stood back, terribly, utterly still.

Time stopped.

The rain hammered on the road, but it seemed to come from a great distance. Heller felt his heart freeze and vomit rose into his throat.

Rage and grief tore through him.

No. No. No! No, no, no, no! NO! NOOOOOOOOOO! his mind screamed.

She slumped out of the cab, arms dangling. Vacant eyes gazed up at Heller. What was left of her face hung upside down.

Heller took her in his arms and slid her limp body out of the cab. He dropped hard on his knees, squeezing her body to his chest as he cradled her head in his arms. He heard the cursing shriek echo through his brain. He clamped his eyes shut and his face contorted in misery. His body shook.

The rain lashed off Jesse Heller's face, whipped away a steady flow of silent tears.

*T*HUNDER RANG OUT. Lightning flashed, parting the night. Rain splattered off the rocks.

Jesse Heller stood atop the high hill like a dark statue. The 12-gauge pump shotgun fisted in his left hand hung low by his side. Rainwater drenched his clothes; it had already washed the blood and the dirt off his face and arms.

But the cold lash of water hadn't eased the pain that burned in his gut.

A haunted, hollow gaze showed in his deep-set eyes. He could just barely discern the flashing lights of squad cars and rescue teams two miles in the distance. A helicopter's search beam knifed the blackness. But the search chopper flew east, away from Jesse Heller.

He knew what they would find down there in the pit of hell, in the ruins of madness.

A terrible, jaded sorrow settled over him. He thought about her, wondered. . . .

Slowly he turned around, limping as he faded into the maw of night. Her memory became another ghost in his mind.

Jesse Heller knew tomorrow would bring another kind of war.

And he feared that there would be still other ghosts.

The man named Hell became a shadow vanishing behind the gray downpour.

Watch for

THE GUNS OF HELL

next in the HELLRIDER series
from Pinnacle Books

coming in December!